Notes Toward the Story

and

Other Stories

[Corey Mesler]

For
Cynthia —
a true believer,
a true
friend

xo Corey
9/17/11

Published by Aqueous Books
P.O. Box 12784
Pensacola, FL 32591
www.aqueousbooks.com
All rights reserved.
Published in the United States of America
ISBN: 978-0-9826734-6-1
First edition, Aqueous Books printing, July 2011
Cover art: Jeane Umbreit www.jeaneumbreit.com
Book design and layout: Cynthia Reeser

Aqueous Books

for John Grisham

Books by Corey Mesler:

Poetry

For Toby, Everything for Toby (1997) Wing & The Wheel Press
Ten Poets (1999) (Ed.) Wing & The Wheel Press
Piecework (2000) Wing & The Wheel Press
Chin-Chin in Eden (2003) Still Waters Press
Dark on Purpose (2004) Little Poem Press
The Hole in Sleep (2006) Wood Works Press
The Agoraphobe's Pandiculations (2006) Little Poem Press
The Lita Conversation (2006) Southern Hum
The Chloe Poems (2007) Maverick Duck Press
Some Identity Problems (2007) Foothills Publishing
Pictures from Lang and Fellini (2007) Sheltering Pines Press
Grit (2008) Amsterdam Press
The Tense Past (2010) Flutter Press
Before the Great Troubling (2010) Unbound Content
The Heart is Open (2011) Right Hand Pointing

Prose

Talk: A Novel in Dialogue (2002) Livingston Press
We Are Billion-Year-Old Carbon (2005) Livingston Press
Short Story and Other Short Stories (2006) Parallel Press
Following Richard Brautigan (chapbook) (2006) Plan B Press
Publisher (2007) Writers Write Journal Press
Listen: 29 Short Conversations (2009) Brown Paper Press
The Ballad of the Two Tom Mores (2010) Bronx River Press
Following Richard Brautigan (full-length novel) (2010) Livingston Press
Listen: 29 Short Conversations (2009) Brown Paper Press
The Ballad of the Two Tom Mores (2010) Bronx River Press
Following Richard Brautigan (full-length novel) (2010) Livingston Press
The Narcoleptic Therapist (2011) Achilles Chapbook Series

Advance Praise for Notes Toward the Story:

Here is a collection of mischief and delight. Corey Mesler's short fictions afford a peek into a parallel universe in which we find ourselves reflected in new and surprising disguises. At times his writing evokes the subversive surrealism of Flann O'Brien and at others the lyrical dreamscapes of Richard Brautigan, but Mesler is always his own man, with a sharp ear for dialogue and a steady eye on the wobbling orbit of modern life. *Notes Towards the Story and Other Stories* may easily become one of your favourite bedside companions.
—Miles Gibson, author of *The Sandman* and *Hotel Plenti*

Corey Mesler's stories give shimmer and depth to the most outlandish and commonplace of experiences. By turns piercingly funny and sneakily heartrending, *Notes Toward the Story and Other Stories* touches the real corners of life while also showing, with great tenderness, the way we seek to elevate ourselves, our condition, the everydayness of our everyday lives, to a level of epic grandeur. And Mesler shows us how the effort itself—the sincerity of it, the yearning behind it—becomes the grandest thing of all.
—Megan Abbott, author of *Bury Me Deep* and *The End of Everything*

These otherworldly stories left me haunted not just by their strange happenings but by the longing that suffuses them. A woman who has her shadow dyed , a child who can't resist the allure of the dark space behind a door—Corey Mesler's characters glimpse a mysterious and terrible beauty in the world, and reading these stories I glimpsed it, too.

—Leah Stewart, author of *The Myth of You and Me* and *Husband and Wife*

A remarkably unique collection that both invokes and takes you away from everyday life—part Raymond Carver, part Gabriel Garcia Márquez. Spare, rich, real, surprising, and absolutely wonderful.
—Jennifer Paddock, author of *A Secret Word* and *Point Clear*

Human nature is pretty shoddy stuff, and we all need forgiveness and
redemption and upward of a thousand second chances.
–Peter DeVries

Keep the story straight and you'll get involved.
–Richard Farina

A Table of Contents

Monster

Prior to the monster taking Effie Sempsh into the woods on August 21st, some things had happened in Effie's life that require delineating. Effie was a complex woman and, though the temptation to simplify her story is strong, in the end truth must be served and details brought to light.

Effie and her husband, Robert Sempsh, lived in a neighborhood not far from the airport, not far from the chemical plants, the kind of neighborhood one passes in one's car and either turns away from or notices with only half one's attention. Nondescript is perhaps descriptive. Rundown, certainly.

Robert worked at a bottling plant in nearby Millington. They produced a lesser-known soft drink, something called Flip, a mixture of citrusy extracts and corn syrup. Robert was not a boss. He was a drone on the line and he hated every single day he worked there. We could say more about Robert, but you probably know his type. Perhaps you went to high school with someone like him. Robert drank. Robert was lazy. Robert abused his wife with an acid tongue and an unassailable sense of his own superiority.

Effie was not happy that she had married Robert. When they were younger he seemed exciting, a sort of poor man's James Dean. Soon, it became clear that his anarchic charm was thin like a coating of sweat, and that he was self-centered and mean. Effie contemplated leaving him, of course. But she was afraid. Robert could get violent, though, so far, he had never hit Effie. He'd broken things, thrown bottles, put his fist through a bedroom door, kicked the neighbor's dog, but he had never hit Effie. Instead he spoke to her as if he hated her. Some part of Robert, some underdeveloped part of Robert, thought that this was how husbands treated wives. Effie never thought so. She thought Robert was unhappy with his life and his unhappiness took the form of mental abuse and coarseness and alcoholism and drug taking.

Effie's father used to hit her. He called her whore and tramp because she had sex with boys in cars. Effie's father was a Baptist preacher.

Effie's best friend, Tammy Northern, lived across the street in a house only a modicum nicer than Effie's. Tammy's husband had taken off a few years ago, leaving her with an infant daughter, Rebecca, and a house note. He had taken their only car, a Yugo. Yet, Tammy did not lie down and die. Instead she took classes at a vo-tech to become a veterinary assistant. She now made pretty good money, drove a new Volkswagen, and kept herself and Becca in most of what is called the necessities. Tammy's home was a pretty happy place to visit, it seemed to Effie, and Effie took advantage, escaping her own plight with long lunches at the Northerns'. Also, Effie loved Becca, little butterball with jet black hair and bush-baby eyes, and often, happily, babysat for her. For this she would not take Tammy's money.

Naturally, Effie envied Tammy her life as a single mom and independent operator. Often before falling asleep at night she imagined such a life for herself. What profession would she like to try? Would she like to date numerous eligible bachelors? Would she, eventually, like to also be a mother? This self-interview was like counting sheep for Effie. After a few minutes of interrogation she would slip gently into Morpheus' tender clench, the god of dreams deferred.

About the same time the monster was first sighted Robert increased the intensity and frequency of his abuse. A couple times, after cursing and throwing things failed to sate his ire, he raised his fist and wondered in that frozen second what it would feel like to strike Effie's once-pretty face. Effie stared at that fist and grew more tired and grew more afraid and felt more trapped than ever.

The monster was first reported in Shelbyville, a town about thirteen miles up Highway 69. Three kids, age ten, twelve, and twelve, were camping in the woods near their home and were awakened by a loud rustling and grunting that sounded like a wild boar. They slowly unzipped their tent expecting to come face to face with a bear, or boar, or panther. Instead they saw an erect creature with the feathery head of a cockatoo, the orange body hair of an ape, the shoulders of a linebacker, and a face as hideous as a nightmare. There were tusks protruding from its slobbery mouth, a nose like an anteater's, and eyes as read as a devil's. This was how the boys described the monster to the police. And they further reported how the thing stood stock-still when they emerged from their tent, caught reaching into the ashy vestiges of their campfire for burnt pieces of hotdog or marshmallow. And, the boys said, the thing seemed frightened of them and scurried off into the woods, running upright like a gorilla, but with the speed of an ocelot.

"Did you see this story about the creature in Shelbyville?" Tammy asked Effie over morning coffee. "Kids."

"Yeah. Probably about as real as Bigfoot and Nessie. Years from now the boys will admit to manufacturing their ogre, just like the Nessie photograph is now known to be a fake."

"Probly," Tammy agreed.

"Of course our woods are dark and deep. No telling what all could be living up in there," Effie added, being, as usual, of two minds.

"Yeah. Maybe a beast like in that Disney cartoon. A scary beast but ultimately sweet," Tammy said. And then, giggling, added, "And really well-hung you'd have to think."

"It would be an upgrade for me," Effie said, and the two women laughed together, sipping coffee, nibbling scones, and then moving on to other topics of interest.

A week later another sighting, this time right in Millington, raised the level of consternation, as well as the level of fear. A busboy for Peter and Samuel's Restaurant, who was working the early morning shift, opened the back door of the restaurant to empty the trash and startled a creature going through their dumpster. The busboy said it was a good eight-feet tall, hairy as an ape, and ugly as a scarecrow. He (it) glared momentarily at the frozen busboy, then turned and ran in the direction of the nearby coppice. He also said the creature was fast. "Like Rajon Rondo."

Now everyone was talking about the monster. Tammy shrugged when Effie asked her what she thought. "Can it be real?" Effie asked.

"Sure. What the hell," Tammy said, turning a couple pancakes in a small frying pan. "You ever seen a crocodile up close? We'd call that a monster if we had never seen it before."

"I guess," Effie said.

"You know Bert, Bert Pipkin, lives in the cove?"

"Um," Effie said, but Tammy was moving on.

"Bert teaches at the university. Maybe he doesn't anymore. He's a real smart man. He teaches anthropology. I think. Maybe it's archeology. Or zoology. Anyway. Bert says folktales often have real-life something or others. Correlations?"

"Huh," Effie said.

"Yeah, Bert says there's always a little grain of truth in any myth. Like sailors thinking narwhals were mermaids. Or was it unicorns?"

"I think I've seen Bert," Effie said, now. "He wear suspenders?"

"Yeah," Tammy laughed. "That's Bert."

"I think I talked to him once," Effie said.

Effie had indeed once talked to the neighborhood rascal, Bert. The way the old guy looked at her made Effie's heart go kerplunk. He was the sort of man who didn't disguise his baser instincts, yet managed to, somehow, not seem a masher. Effie was embarrassed the morning she went to the mailbox and Bert was in the street, cursing and pulling at the tangled whipcord of his weed whacker. She was embarrassed because she was wearing a rock band (Whitesnake) T-shirt and plum sweatpants. Yet, she thought, why should it matter if this stranger, this eccentric old man with his Godspell suspenders, sees her in sweatpants?

Bert came over to her.

"Sorry about my language, Mrs. Sempsh," Bert said. "Goddamn weed whacker." And he laughed.

Effie laughed, too.

They stood and grinned at each other. It was obvious Bert didn't care that she was in sweatpants. It was obvious because he couldn't take his eyes off her braless breasts and their neat little nipples showing through her T-shirt. Effie was stirred. It had been a long time since Effie had been stirred. And by this inappropriate neighbor, for goodness' sake. How old must he be, seventy?

"I'm Bert Pipkin," Bert said and put out a thin, strong hand, with gnarly veins. Effie took the hand and found the man's skin surprisingly soft.

"Effie Sempsh," Effie said and then laughed again. He obviously knew her name.

"Effie," Bert said. His eyes were tickling her nipples.

"Okay," Effie said. "See ya." And she went back inside her house.

Later it occurred to her that she had forgotten her mail. She would have to return to the box after Bert went inside. She sat in her living room staring at the TV, which was off. She was stirred. I'm not dead yet, she thought.

The third time the monster made the news was a week after the restaurant sighting. This time he boldly came into someone's backyard. And this was only a half-mile or so from Effie's house. The monster had made off with the family's dog.

"He's getting closer," Tammy said, smiling and stirring her coffee.

"I know," Effie said. She was a bit distracted. She had found a rubber in Robert's pants pocket that morning while doing laundry. Why was Robert carrying rubbers? The answer was obvious.

"Bert says he's genuine but he doesn't like the term *monster*. Bert said, 'Be careful who you're calling a monster. The real monsters might object.'"

"Robert is a real monster," Effie said, matter-of-factly.

"Another fight?" Tammy asked, her face now all concern.

"Not yet," Effie said and she managed a sardonic grin.

That evening during dinner Effie pulled the rubber out of her pocket and placed it next to Robert's plate, alongside his knife and fork.

"What's that?" Robert said.

"I think you know what it is, Robert."

"You wanna fuck?" he asked. It was the sort of trashy swagger that turned Effie's stomach. She wanted to spit.

"Why are you carrying rubbers in your pockets?" she asked, trying to keep her voice composed. Tears were marshalling behind her eyelids.

Robert looked at her. He picked up the rubber and held the package in the palm of his hand. He looked at it as if it were a small toy. He smiled at Effie and stuck the rubber in his pants pocket. "Bring me dinner," he said.

"Robert," Effie said. "Why are you carrying a goddamn rubber?"

It was then that Robert hit Effie for the first time. He backhanded her as neatly as a gunslinger pulling a gun. Effie's nose shot out a bright upsurge of blood. She ran to the bathroom and locked the door. Robert sat still for a moment. Then he stood and got his own food.

So now it is complete, Effie thought. I have gone from my father's fist to my husband's. Some kind of evil circle has completed itself.

The next morning, after Robert had gone to work, Effie made her solitary way to her friend's house. She wanted comfort but she didn't want to talk about her nose, now red with what looked like a black streak through it, as if someone had drawn there with lipstick and an eyebrow pencil.

"Oh, Jesus!" Tammy screeched. "That bastard!"

She led Effie into the house by the elbow as if she suspected that Effie might be wobbly on her pins from being popped on the whiffer. In the kitchen Bert Pipkin sat at Tammy's table, a cup of coffee in front of him. On one of his suspenders was a button, like a "Your Name Here" badge at a school reunion. The button said, *Think Green.*

"What happened, Mrs. Sempsh?" Bert said, his voice warm and caressing.

"Please call me Effie," Effie said, sitting down across from him. Bert reached over and touched the back of her hand. The gesture was affectionate, friendly. Bert's eyes, Effie noticed now, were blue with a light rim of water as if he could cry at any moment. He was still a very attractive man, leonine and assured. Tammy had told Effie that Bert had lived on their street since he was a young newlywed. He had owned that house for most of his life and had watched the neighborhood slowly deteriorate. He retired from the local university five years ago.

"I tripped over our throw rug," Effie said to the room.

Tammy said, "I'll kill that bastard. I swear I will."

"Tammy," Effie said.

"Bert, will you kill her slimeball husband for me? I mean it, will you?"

"Does he hit you often?" Bert said, again in soothing, warm tones.

"No, no," Effie said a bit too quickly. "He's never hit me before. I mean, he has a temper but—" And here Effie began to sob quietly. Bert and Tammy watched her for a moment to see if she could collect herself.

Tammy sat next to her and put a hand on her shoulder.

"He's trash, Bert," Tammy now said. "He's just trash."

The monster was next seen that afternoon, moving along the edge of the wooded area two streets over from Effie's. He looked like a man in a hurry, a large, hairy man. He glanced toward the small group of people who stood stock-still watching him. No one spoke.

Then suddenly the monster was gone. He had disappeared into a gap in the woods the way a mouse becomes two-dimensional to squeeze into your house. The sylvan darkness swallowed him, *blip*.

Finally someone spoke.

"Should we go get some hunters or somebody, some guns, and go after that thing?" someone said. It was the beginning of something impure, something precarious. It was the beginning of the contagious idea that their neighborhood, as run-down as it was, was in danger, and no amount of vigilance or level of retaliation would be an overreaction.

The morning of August 21st was like most mornings at the Sempsh home. A few days ago Robert had apologized for his smack to Effie's face. He had apologized, as they say, in his way.

In his way.

That's what I am, thought Effie. Just something else he has to move around to gain the things he wants from the world: another drink, food prepared for him, a fresh-faced fuck every once in a while.

Effie set Robert's pancakes and sausage in front of him on the morning of August 21st. She put the preserves and syrup within his reach. He barely looked at her. Food arrived for Robert as if pixie-borne.

Effie's nose now was the yellow of a dull bug light. "Yellow as a hopeless lover," Effie's Aunt Pat used to say.

"The coffee's not very hot," Robert said, after a while. He was reading the paper, the news on August 21st. Effie was leaning against the sink, chewing on a cuticle, staring out across their small yard at the rubbish in the small yard backing up to theirs.

Effie looked at her husband. There was hot coffee on the stove. Admittedly, she was closer to it. Effie gave a moment's thought to throwing the coffee in her husband's face. Instead she wearily hoisted the pot and topped off Robert's cup. He didn't move or say a word. He was reading another article about the monster. This morning's editorial speculated that he was more akin to the Yeti than to Bigfoot. The distinction was a fine one, it seemed.

That afternoon, at home alone, Effie found herself staring out her front window. She had been listless all day. She had wandered from room to room like a stink. She was moony and sad.

Outside she saw Bert Pipkin digging around the base of his mailbox. His thin old back showed a semicircle of perspiration on his carmine shirt. There was something about that arc of sweat that attracted Effie. She woke up.

Effie found herself in the bedroom looking frantically through drawers. She had to hurry. Bert could go inside any moment. What Effie chose to put on was a pair of thin running shorts, her briefest panties, and a T-shirt with cut-off arms. Before putting the shirt on Effie removed her bra. She willed her nipples to stand at attention. She wanted Bert to see those nipples. Effie had a fine new idea, one that had been brewing for a while. She was going to fuck Bert Pipkin.

In the bathroom Effie put in her diaphragm. She was wet. She was surprised at how wet she was already. She actually smiled at herself in the mirror. This was something she could do. She was not dead. She could still have sex.

Leaving the bathroom in a rush she ran into her husband, home unexpectedly. She hit his chest and fell backward as if she had tripped or been thrown aside. Robert looked at his wife in her short shorts and skimpy T-shirt. He studied her for a second. Then he saw the diaphragm case open on the back of the toilet. In her haste Effie had left it there.

Robert grabbed Effie by the hair. Effie did not scream. Robert slapped her once. Effie took it. She was guilty. She was about to be punished.

Robert practically dragged his wife into the kitchen. He threw her down into a chair. Then he went to the silverware drawer and began to rummage. He was looking for something but he did not know what. Something heavy, something that would hurt his wife but not kill her. He found a wooden, mace-like object. It had a flanged head. He didn't know what it was used for but it fit his hand like a weapon.

He turned toward Effie, who sat in the chair, slump-shouldered and afraid. Tears ran down her cheeks. Effie saw the mallet, the meat tenderizer.

"No, Robert," she said, quietly. But she knew it was too late to protest. It was years too late.

Robert walked toward his wife. He hit her once with the back of his hand. Effie put a hand to her cheek but otherwise did not move. She did not raise her hands to protect herself.

"Who?" Robert said, raising the weapon. "Who?"

Effie looked up at him. What did it matter, she said in her head.

"Who?" Robert said, and swung the mace, once, halfheartedly. It met the side of Effie's head with a dull sound and she was deafened. There was a roar inside her. It was her blood answering her attacker.

Effie was not sure quite what happened next. Suddenly a darkness crossed their kitchen window, a strong, angry cloud. She did not hear the back door wrenched open. Suddenly Robert was not standing in front of her any longer. Blood ran into Effie's eyes.

Robert was not standing in front of her any longer. The monster had picked him up and thrown him out the back door. The monster had then gone out into the yard for a few minutes, maybe two or three. Effie sat in the chair. Her hand was caressing her sore cheek, her fingers now coated in blood. She did not know what was happening. She was dizzy. She was perhaps hallucinating.

The monster returned and lifted Effie. He gently swung her over his shoulder. As they exited the house the monster stepped over Robert, lying at the bottom of the steps, mired in mud and blood. Robert had landed on the cheap lawn sprinkler and now it bent around his head like a cracked headset. It looked comic and cheerless. Robert watched the monster carry his wife away but Robert could not move. Broken bones were involved. Robert watched the monster take his wife into the woods. They disappeared into the darkness of the woods as if they had walked through a door into another dimension.

"Fuck," Robert said, right before he passed out.

Slung over the monster's shoulder Effie was surprisingly calm. She thought about an expression she had heard, something about the devil you know versus the devil you do not. She didn't want to know the devil she knew anymore.

Effie had no idea how long she rode that great bony shoulder. She may have swooned, or dozed. It seemed as if they had travelled miles. She did not know the wooded area near her home was so deep, so dark, so tangled, and spackled with only tiny spears of sunlight. The monster moved swiftly but smoothly. Effie felt as if she were gliding, flying.

On they went. For miles they went.

Effie let her hands, which dangled over the creature's back, feel the muscular landscape beneath its matted fur. He was a powerful animal.

Some time later, an hour, a day, the monster stopped. The groundcover was thick and extraordinary. Effie thought she couldn't possibly be in the woods near her home, the plain, kudzuey, Southern woods she had grown up with. All around her was a lush explosion of greenery, thick and twisted and strange. It was a nightmare's forest, a place of florid black magic, except that Effie was calm, was unafraid.

The monster had stopped near the base of an enormous tree, an oak perhaps. Effie wished she knew plant life. The tree was thick and covered with gnarly, shaggy vines, thick vines that wound around the trunk like constrictors. The beast readjusted Effie on his shoulder. His strong hand on her back felt reassuring, even affectionate. Effie thought she might swoon again.

Then as sudden as the crack of a rifle the monster grasped a vine and began to move upward at an expeditious clip. He was carrying Effie into the trees. They rose like a column of smoke, swiftly and smoothly into the darkness near the top. The leaves, damp with nature, slid across Effie's cheeks and arms. She felt bedewed, refreshed. And still up they went. It got darker.

Until they came to a stopping point. The monster set her down. She was standing on a plank floor. She was standing on a solid oak plank floor. Her eyes widened in amazement. Above her she could see treetop, the sun a dappling brightness through the arabesque of foliage. She was on the porch of a house, a house built in the trees. It was small but beautifully made. Everything, door to hinge, boards to logs, window to wall, was finely connected. It was gorgeous. Effie tentatively stepped inside. There was an actual door! The monster moved backward, slowly, cautiously. He was afraid to let her see.

She stood in the middle of the room, amid rugs and handmade furniture and oil lamps and cooking stove and bookshelves (bookshelves!), and she was positively dizzy with what she was witnessing. She turned her wide-eyed wonder toward the monster. She smiled encouragement. Finally, she found her voice.

"Did you, did you build this?" Effie asked, tentatively, as if speaking to a child. "I'm sorry, can you understand me?"

"Yes," the monster said. He cleared his jumbo throat. "I understand you. Though I am out of practice conversing."

"You—you," Effie didn't know what she wanted to say. "You—saved me."

"Mm," the monster said. "He seemed a very bad man."

"He's an awful man, yes," Effie said, and suddenly felt shy before this creature, so colossal and strong and exotic.

"I hurt him," the monster said.

"Yes," Effie said and she smiled sweetly at him.

"I don't understand," Effie said, after a while. "You talk, you build, you—you read! Where did you come from?"

The monster looked sad. He put a large hand on a globe and spun it absentmindedly.

"I'm sorry," Effie said. "It doesn't matter."

"Sit," the monster said.

Effie sat on the couch, her legs drawn beneath her.

The monster also sat on the couch. His hair was thick like a cross between a boar's and an orangutan's. And it smelled slightly like wet leather, or creosote, a musky but not unpleasant funk.

"I'm sorry, I don't know your name," Effie said. "Mine is Effie."

"Effie," he said. And for a second she thought he meant it was his name, too.

"I am called, was called, Genet."

Now it was Effie's turn to repeat. "Genet." She said it softly the way one might pronounce the name of a magical place, a new Eden.

In the days that followed Genet and Effie became closer. She could cook some things he could not. He brought her squirrels and possums and snakes. She improvised meals that pleased them both. Gradually a warmth grew between them. Effie almost forgot about her life down below. She was enchanted, captivated if not captured.

Some nights they sat on the couch holding hands and talking about their past lives. Effie still never understood where Genet had come from. He would only speak about it in vague terms as if it had passed away into myth, like Atlantis. He seemed lost, out of his element. He had taken to eating trash. Was he a victim like her?

And as they grew closer it was inevitable that they should finally share one bed. Effie had often been nude in front of her host (there was little privacy in their small quarters), but nothing sexual had arisen from it. But on this night, as if by mutual agreement, they ended up in the same bed. Genet was modest, reticent. He told her he had not been with a woman in over ten years. Where had he lived then, Effie wondered. Effie wondered if he meant a human woman like her. Effie allowed she was pretty sexually pent-up herself.

They lay under the thin cotton sheet for a while. Effie's nakedness was stimulating her giant friend. He seemed impatient now, and a low growl rumbled through him.

"Genet," she whispered in his ear.

"I'm not a monster," Genet said. "I am just a very ugly man."

And, at that moment, I wish I could tell you that Effie found him beautiful, but it was not so. He was hideous, as ugly as a devil born of mud.

But it didn't matter. She reached down and felt for his pizzle. It was already erect and as big and thick as a horse's. My stars, she thought, if Tammy could see me now. And right before she mounted the monster Effie wondered if she had put in her diaphragm. But then, in an incandescent flash of epiphany and joy and optimism and prescience, she thought to herself, it does not matter. He is my one lover now.

Killer

My dog's name is Killer, but, really, it was meant ironically. We named him that when a pup. He's a spitz/Akita mix, a funny-looking dog, built like a small bull. He weighs about fifty-five pounds and is all muscle.

He slipped the leash. That's what happened. The next thing I knew he was in someone's yard and going crazy. It was too dark for me to see properly what he was after, but I found him in the hedge with an orange cat pinned in the corner. Killer was fierce—I'd never seen him like that—and the cat was hissing like a cat in the wild.

The guy came onto his porch to see what the din was—it was an unnaturally warm night for January—and he immediately began to swear at Killer and try to shoo him away, keeping his distance, I have to laugh. I began to apologize profusely, while trying to grab Killer by the scruff of his neck, but he was too strong.

The cat made a run for it, disappearing into a narrow vent under the house. And damned if Killer didn't go right in after it. I didn't think he'd fit—that would be his comeuppance, getting his ass stuck under there. The owner of the cat was standing beside me now—in a T-shirt and pajama bottoms—and his expression was grim. He was teetering between being neighborly and getting on his high horse. I know the type.

We could hear the animals under there—the sounds were almost unearthly, what a ruckus. I could make out Killer's snarling exhalations—either he was stuck under the plumbing, or he'd gotten the cat cornered.

I looked at the cat's owner and said, "I'm sorry about this."

"Things happen," he said, not meeting my eyes.

Fuck him.

Then there was the voice of a child coming from the guy's backyard. I think the cat had slipped out a narrow vent on the far side.

"She's okay," the kid yelled.

"Well, good," I said to the guy, who now was running his hand through his uncombed hair. Like he had the weight of the world on him.

"All's well that ends well, ay?" I said.

"Yeah," he offered. Then, as an afterthought, he stuck out his hand. I shook it.

"Your dog," he said.

I don't know whether it was concern or remonstration he was after because just then Killer came skulking out from under the house. He hunkered down to get through the opening.

"There he is," I said, and then to pacify the homeowner, "You nasty boy."

I leashed him and smiled at the guy. He smiled back and gave me a halfhearted one-hand salute.

I waved back.

Killer and I walked home in the dark. Killer wasn't pulling on the leash anymore the way he does at the start of every walk. He seemed worn-out or perhaps satisfied in some canine way.

When we got back home my wife, Karina, was watching *Friends*. She half-turned toward us.

"Good walk?" she said.

I wanted to whip her with the leash such was my rage at her indifference. I wanted to demand—I don't know what. Wasted emotions, my shrink calls them.

In the kitchen I got Killer a Milk-Bone. He took it as his due.

I sat on the floor and wrestled him forcefully, holding his ruff. He growled, playacting; it was part of our relationship. I let out a long sigh, one that had begun to build in me at that asshole's house.

It was then that I noticed the blood around Killer's mouth. A smart red smudge like an eloquent flame.

Jim Cherry in the Otherworld

> "Meet me, Jesus, meet me.
> Oh, won't you meet me in the middle of the air.
> And if my wings should fail me
> Won't you provide me with another pair."
>
> –Traditional, from "Bury My Body"

On the second day, when Jim Cherry's chest pains continued, he began to contemplate his own mortality.

Not that Jim hadn't thought about death before; in fact, thoughts of death were Jim's comrades, his familiars. He had always felt fragile, insubstantial, as ethereal as a soap bubble. It was the consequence, he believed, of reading too many depressing novels in those formative years, the early twenties.

Now, here he was, forty-two, married, and with two small children. It was marriage, fatherhood, which saved Jim from a life spent in contemplation of his own navel, so to speak, a life of self-absorption and egocentric anxiety. He had "grown up," as his wife, Sharilyn, told him. He had quieted his "inner child."

And it was true, distaste for this kind of self-help psychobabble aside. Jim Cherry was a man, if not exactly whole (how many of us are?), then at a sort of cease-fire stage with his demons. Formerly overwrought, even on the best of days, he now had times of mental leisure and happiness, times spent enjoying the nearby burble and whir of his children at play, content to laze in the La-Z-Boy while his family ebbed and flowed around him. This was a good time for Jim and he knew it, and by knowing it compounded his sense of ease.

That morning, he called his wife from the travel agency where he worked, with a slight feeling of foreboding, but nothing, he felt, which would disrupt the stream of everydayness.

"What's up," Jim began, with a frail buoyancy. Something like dyspepsia pinged beneath his sternum.

"I talked to Japan this morning. Japan. I am still of an age to marvel at that," Sharilyn said. Sharilyn worked for a small publisher of children's books and, in her daily routine, used faxes, e-mail, and the Internet, but technology constantly remained a source of wonder to her.

"I talked to Jackie," Jim deadpanned. "Just like that. Just opened up and spoke to him. How about that?"

"Go ahead. Be sportive."

"I don't feel right," Jim now said.

"What do you mean, right?"

"Funny."

"You don't feel funny? You're funny enough."

"No, I feel funny. Not right. Maybe a pain in my chest."

"Really?"

"Yeah. A slight pain. Gas maybe?"

"Probably. Do you think you ought to go to the emergency room?"

"Nah. Gas probably. I got some stuff to do here."

"You sure?"

"Yeah."

"Well, call me back if it gets worse. Call me back anyway."

"All right. Go talk to Somalia or someplace. Where's Somalia?"

"I don't know. Love you."

When Jim got home that night neither he nor Sharilyn mentioned the pain in Jim's chest. Sharilyn put it down to more hypochondria, more unnecessary worry. After all, she had endured years of Jim's neurotic responses to the world.

About eight o'clock Jim's chest pain was slightly more pronounced and he brought it up again.

"Jim, maybe you ought to go have it checked out. They say not to mess around with chest pain."

"Yeah, I know. Maybe I'll just go to the minor emergency clinic."

"You had such a bad experience there last time."

"I know. What's the chances of getting that quack again?"

"Pretty good, I'd say."

"Nah, I'll just go there. It's right around the corner."

Nathan, their six-year-old, tumbled in just then.

"Where you going, Pop?"

"Just up to the doctor. Nothing to worry about."

Jim drove himself to the clinic with some trembling in his limbs. He hated these "Doc in a Box" places, with their peremptory approach to care.

The doctor there that evening was indeed the same one as before. His misdiagnosis of an infection had led to some hospital time.

"What's the problem, Mr. Cherry?" the runty, pompous physician said as he swept into the examining room.

"Just some minor chest pains." Jim managed a tight smile.

"No such thing. You're gonna have to go to the emergency room. I'm not equipped to handle chest pain here."

"Just like that?"

"Yep. Jim, I can examine you and run you through some tests, bill you for it, but in the end I'm gonna send you to the hospital. Your choice."

"Well, hell. I'll just go."

"Right, I'll take your name off the books here."

Jim sat in his car and fretted. He didn't want to go to the emergency room. He wanted to go home and kiss his kids good night and get in bed with his willowy wife and read his James Cain novel and sleep on his own pillow. But, knowing himself, knowing his worry would escalate, he drove the mile or so to the midtown emergency room and parked his car in the pay lot.

From a phone just inside the door he called Sharilyn.

"They sent me to the emergency room."

"Jim. Why did they do that?"

"Oh, it was that little jerk again. He couldn't take the responsibility so he passed on me. It's all *save my own ass* in the medical field. Anyway, here I am. I'm fixing to get probed."

"You want me to come down? I can get Ruth to pop over and stay with the kids."

"Nah. I'll be here a while, I'm sure. I'll call you."

But Jim made it through the labyrinth of hospital procedure surprisingly quickly, and rather than an overnight stay, which Jim had anticipated as a matter of course, he was released a few hours later, with the assuagement of a diagnosis of pleurisy.

Still, Jim was alarmed by the evening's disarray, and did not trust, that, just like that, he was back among the unscathed, the sturdy.

Sharilyn was reading in bed when Jim got home. The house was as still as a moored ship, and this was Jim's favorite time of day, when the children were safe in bed and the house was quiet and he and Sharilyn were chatting about the day's particulars, about the books they were reading, about the tiny progressions their kids were making in their voyages out into the world. It was a time of peace and reassurance.

"Whad they say?" she asked immediately.

"Pleurisy." Jim smiled.

"Well. Thank God."

"Yeah."

"What do you do for that?"

"Take souped-up Midol apparently."

"Well, that's a relief."

"Yes."

"I'm glad you're home. I thought for sure they'd keep you overnight."

"Me too, both things. Man, they respond quickly when you use the phrase 'chest pains.' They don't mess around."

"I'm glad."

"Yes. Kids okay? Angie's scrape healing up?"

"Yeah. Katy said she talked about it all day, though. Sort of a trauma and a badge of honor simultaneously."

"Ha. Nathan go to sleep all right?"

"Usual skirmish. He dropped off, though, in the middle of *Ozma of Oz*."

"You tired? You gonna read some more?"

"No, I'm beat. I was just waiting up to hear from you. You?"

"I'm gonna have to read. I'm a little wired, anxious. You want me to go in the other room?"

"No. I'm so zonked the light won't bother me."

"Good night, then."

Jim Cherry was not overly secure about the doctor's prognosis and his doubt was not misplaced. Jim died that night in his sleep of what they said was a major infarction. He passed away quietly with his willowy wife beside him and his children safe in their beds and his dreams full of medical procedures and women from his past and long, winding hallways like sets from Caligari, leading into more passageways, slanting and ominous, and eventually into darkness.

*

Jim Cherry's arrival in the afterlife was as uneventful as any of the tens of thousands of other arrivals that night, but to Jim it was a circumstance of major significance. Suddenly, he was no longer in the confusing landscape of dream, but, instead, standing in a long waiting line, behind a fat science fiction fan from St. Joseph, Iowa, and in front of a wizened old woman from Lima, Peru. Jim blinked a few times at the solidity of his surroundings, the linoleum floor, the plastered walls, the claustrophobia of the hall down which the queue wound. There was something antiseptic, officious, about the corridor, like a corridor in a public building. The transition from dream to reality, if reality this was, was seamless, and Jim was understandably disconcerted. "What the hell?" he muttered, craning his neck down the line.

"Let's hope not," the bespectacled fatty said, not even looking up from his E.E. "Doc" Smith novel, whose cover bore the expected buxom space princess in scanty attire.

"Are we dead?" Jim asked, in a voice already small, but made smaller by the echoless enclosure of the hallway.

"Seems so," the man now said, looking over his glasses at Jim for the first time.

"Damn."

"You must stop assuming the worst," the man said and smiled. Jim discovered he was joking. He was dead and joking.

Jim shuffled forward with the other anesthetized deceased. He felt disembodied, not exactly at ease but not exactly apprehensive either. A heavy lethargy pulled at his limbs and he could only manage to move forward a scoot at a time. His chest pain was gone. He was still in his pajamas.

The longer he stood in line the longer the line behind him grew. Suddenly there was a man in lumberjack attire and then, just as suddenly, a little Asian girl behind him, dressed in a swimming suit. She whimpered quietly at first, but then settled in, moving forward with the same robotic gracelessness as her fellow attendees.

Finally, there were only a handful of people between Jim and the front desk, a sort of raised podium upon which were engraved the words: *Malice toward none, charity toward all.* Jim felt better reading this.

Behind the scrutoir sat a middle-aged man, scribbling in the inevitable ledger. He was dressed like a banker from the 1930s, tight little vest and tie knotted taut against his prominent Adam's apple.

He looked up at Jim as Jim said, "Abraham Lincoln."

The man appeared startled.

"Heh?"

"I said 'Abraham Lincoln.'"

The man looked to his ledger.

"I have here James Fenimore Cherry."

"Oh, right. That's me."

"Then why confuse me?" the man snorted.

"I was commenting on the quote on your desk. It's Abraham Lincoln."

"Sure it is."

"Isn't it?" Jim asked, sheepishly, remembering where he was.

"Mr. Cherry?"

"Right."

"You've completed your life sentence, as you may gather, and you are set now to move on."

"Is this heaven?"

"Sure, sure."

"Not the other place?"

"The other place?"

"Um, hell, you know."

"Sure, sure."

"It is?"

"Is what?"

"Hell."

"Mr. Cherry, this is a way station. I am the way station master, Mr. Shrive."

"Ah. So, if I may be so bold, am I set for heaven or hell?"

"These terms are meaningless here in the Otherworld. You will, when we finish here, move on. That's all I can tell you for that's all I know."

"Okay. What do we need to do?"

"Just a few quick questions."

"Uh, Mr. Shrive, before I answer questions, may I ask one?"

"Yes, Mr. Cherry?"

"Is there a chance I might go back?"

"Go back?"

"To the world. To my life."

"Oh. No. No chance. Highly irregular. Not that we don't get asked, but really, Mr. Cherry. It's normally the very young who ask. You were, after all, given 15,447 days. A quite-sufficient time. You were never promised more."

"Yes, I know. But I have young children."

"Hardly unusual, Mr. Cherry. Many die with young children. The little ones, they survive, live quite-productive lives, or not, as the case may be. Nothing to be done about it, leastwise on this end."

"Are you suggesting I could have done something differently, stretched my time out, done more with what I was given?"

"I'm not here for a philosophical discussion. Predestination, all that. Probably a few fewer hotdogs, not so much salt. Who's to say, Mr. Cherry?"

"You, I would think."

"No, no, sir. I am not in that position, not privy to that kind of information. Merely speculation on my part. Now we need to move on. Got quite a few behind you as you can see."

"Yes, but, Mr. Shrive. I didn't finish *Ozma of Oz*. I didn't even kiss Angie good night."

Here Mr. Shrive paused. A slight tremor seemed to run through him and he put down his scrivening tool. A silence fell over the hallway. This was enough to ignite a minute hope in Jim Cherry like a freshly lit pilot light.

"I didn't finish *Ozma of Oz*," he repeated.

JIM CHERRY IN THE OTHERWORLD

When Mr. Shrive spoke again, it was with a small catch in his voice, which he cleared with a cough, as if he were caught being unprofessional.

"Mr. Cherry," he said. "Jim. What would you have us do?"

Jim brightened slightly. "Then there is a process available, a, a way of dealing with exceptions."

"Now, now. Of course, there are provisions. Not that there are mistakes made. Ever. But, occasionally, one runs up upon what we might call circumstantial grace. But, this is rare, Mr. Cherry."

"Jim."

"Jim. Let me make a few things clearer. Let me outline one or two situations, see if that helps us here. One such, ah, exception involves returning as a ghost, a spirit. This, as I said, is rare, but in cases of murder, unnatural catastrophes, etc., occasionally a temporary return visa is granted, and one goes back as a bit of differentiated ether, a preta. Does this appeal to you, uh, Jim?"

Jim hung his head and thought. "Not really, Mr. Shrive. I mean, it might scare the children, traumatize them, hardly what I had in mind."

"Quite."

"So?"

"So, there are few other choices."

"But there are other choices. Please, Mr. Shrive, let's not linger over this. You tease me."

"Mr. Cherry, these things are not done lightly. It is required of me that I make this as exacting as possible. This is not a swinging door."

"Forgive me. It's just that, if there's anything you can do."

"A second procedure returns the deceased to his body shortly after the time of death, but this can be most unpleasant.

Unfortunately, the body, having already died, begins to putrefy, and we have a sort of death-in-life effect, a nosferatu, if you will. Again, not what we would wish upon our children."

"But, a third possibility?"

"Well, Jim," and here Mr. Shrive's voice dipped lower, "There are imperfections with the third procedure, kinks, you see."

"Kinks?"

"Well, in Procedure 3, Antithanatocoenosis, the individual is placed back in the body immediately preceding the moment of delivery—"

"Well, now we're talking, I mean, if you can do that—"

"Mr. Cherry, please. The process is rarely used and there have been a few unfortunate, well..."

"I don't care. It's the only chance I have, yes?"

"It would seem so, in this instance, yes."

"Damn the risks," Jim expostulated.

"Mr. Cherry, please."

*

Jim Cherry awoke next to his willowy wife, whose chocolate hair spread across the pillow beside him like a beautiful stain. She was breathing lightly and he could smell her slightly sour exhalations. It was just before 6 a.m. He knew again the peace of his still and secure domicile; he could almost feel his children, nearby, breathing in their beds.

He pulled the covers from his wife's prone form and bent his face over her sleeping body, inhaling its humanness. He ran a hand over the sheer material of her nightgown and she stirred.

His hands crept up under the nightie and caressed the flesh he had so often caressed before. He ran one hand around the spreading curves of her buttocks with light pressure, while the other ran from breast to breast. He was learning her anew. He was reinvented and reinventing.

He gently parted her legs and she was warm there, and, as always, moist like loam. She opened her eyes with mild surprise and a few moments later smiled in genuine pleasure.

"Mm, Jim, honey," she said and nuzzled her head behind his ear.

"Morning sex. It's been so long," she murmured.

Jim entered his wife and rocked with her like a boat at sea, and when he came he wanted to shout "Hallelujah!"

"Jesus, Jim," Sharilyn said, rolling over. "You flooded me. What are you, eighteen again? You devil, you."

And Jim Cherry ran to his children and swept their sleepy bodies into his arms and acted very much like a man given a second chance at life, throwing love about like poppies and weeping the tears of the just.

The days passed in quick succession for Jim Cherry and, though his daily routine had changed little, he pursued every activity with a sense of purpose pretty much disappeared from human endeavor and with a relish for the smallest joy. His family embraced his new personality and the exhilaration spread like a flu through them and it was as if life had been recast. The world was the world but the Cherrys chased their every dream and lived for every moment and it was bliss, pure and simple, though nothing pure is ever simple and vice versa.

The worm in the apple, if you'll pardon the metaphor, soon became apparent and Jim recognized it for what it was, the flowering of Mr. Shrive's predication.

The case was this: Jim had a trivial though plaguesome affliction in his speech patterns. Specifically, he had trouble using the proper nouns for the objects of the world. Not proper nouns like those with capitals, but the *correct* nouns. He would as easily call an automobile a flyswatter as a flyswatter a waitress. It was disconcerting, in a minor irritation sort of way, and Jim took it in stride. It was a small price to pay.

Early on, Sharilyn was perplexed, even distressed. She feared Jim had developed a brain lesion. It seems she had read something or other about this, perhaps it was in one of Oliver Sacks' books, people who couldn't recognize things for what they were. Or, no, recognized them but couldn't name them.

One morning Sharilyn found Jim cursing in the kitchen and when she asked what the matter was, he looked at her with the stupefaction of a child.

"I was trying to make Nathan a handbill," he said and he looked saddened by his inability to communicate. It was as if he had Alzheimer's.

"Toast," Sharilyn said.

"Yes, toast," Jim said, nodding. "It's exactly that. Toast."

"Jim, what is it? Lately, you seem confused. You're not drinking, are you?"

Jim was almost amused by this misplaced concern.

"Nah. Shar, it's nouns."

"Nouns."

"Right. I can't always count on using the correct one." And then, almost to himself. "An insignificant problem, if that's the worst of it."

And Sharilyn put her arms around him and found the burnt crust which was jamming the toaster and life went on.

But, things began to snowball, communication-wise, and at work especially Jim knew a new embarrassment. He began to see how life must be for the handicapped, the lame, the mentally troubled. The polite looks of bewilderment were weighing.

Once he asked a fellow worker for her epitaph, when all he wanted was to file a hangnail. And, once when Nathan's teacher had called to talk over a minor behavioral problem, Jim had asked if Nathan's penis was a problem for her. He meant handwriting and, understandably, it took some straightening out. From then on, Sharilyn was left in charge of much of the family communication with the workaday world.

It took a while, also, for the children to understand, especially little Angie. Playing Monopoly with Nathan one evening he told his son he owed thirty-four mulligrubs. Nathan looked exasperated as much with his father's inanity as with landing on his property.

"Daddy talks funny," Angie said.

"Sorry," Jim said. "It's those cabbages again."

"Eh?"

"He means nouns, kids," Sharilyn said.

"Nouns, right."

But, as the days went on, this mumpsimus became just another strand of the fabric of their lives, troublesome, annoying, but life was rich and multivariate and Jim Cherry was still inhaling large draughts of rarefied air.

One day at work, as Jim sat at his desk looking over new brochures from the Cayman Islands (apparently there was a city on Grand Cayman Island called Hell and its dead, black, moon surface drew Jim's attention like an omen), Jim's fax began printing a message without the phone having rung. Jim looked at the machine with a sort of dazed half-interest.

He checked the ringer and it was on.

He pulled the weightless page from the machine and, before reading it, put it to his nose and sniffed, just like he used to with his mimeographed tests in school. The effect was Proustian: it smelled exactly like Silly Putty. At the top of the page, in large block letters, was this masthead:

OTHERWORLD, INC.

And the message ran:

Mr. Cherry, please meet me in Overton Park, east playground, bandstand. Today. 1 p.m.

> *Sincerely,*
> *J. Shrive*

Jim was quite surprised by this missive. Perhaps the door between worlds swung a little more freely than Mr. Shrive had let on. Jim could barely repress his jitters, a mix of nervous expectation and fear, until his lunch break. On the drive over to the park he nervously changed radio stations every few notes until he landed on an old Beatles tune, always a balm.

The last chord of "Let it Be" resounded as Jim switched off the engine of his Corolla. From where he parked he could see a phantom figure in the shadowy umbra of the bandstand. Unmistakably it was Mr. Shrive, hunched forward on a bench, tossing crumbs to the strutting and muttering pigeons.

"Saint Francis," Jim said as he approached.

"What?" Mr. Shrive looked startled.

"Forget it," Jim said.

"Thank you for being so prompt," Mr. Shrive said, rising and extending a bony hand.

"Right," Jim said and the two men sat on the spattered bench.

"I imagine my note was a bit of a surprise," Shrive began.

"Quite."

"Not normal procedure, I'm afraid."

Jim contemplated his benefactor with a look of querulous bemusement.

"What's different about my case, then, Mr. Shrive? Am I doing something wrong? Is there a protocol to getting your life back, a proper way of handling renewed mortality?"

"Not in the way you're imagining. And your case, well, it *is* different, Mr. Cherry. I'm afraid there was no good reason to send you back, no overwhelming justification."

"A whim, then. A whim on your part?"

"Not on my part, no. You continue to overestimate my importance. A whim from higher up, to use your vernacular. An experiment, if you will. We've been having so much trouble with Procedure 3, we, that is, others, um, in the Otherworld, decided to give you another go in the hope that we could see our way a little more clearly, in the hope we could refine the program. You are, in a way, helping us. Um, Mr. Cherry."

"Glad to," Jim said with a wink. "Don't mind being a cosmic guinea pig."

"Good. Quite what I hoped you would say. Because there is a little more to the experiment."

"Ah. A catch."

"No, no. It's just that this seems to be going quite well, no, um, glitches that we're aware of..."

"Except my noun problem."

"Oh, yes. Forgot that. Not too troublesome, eh?"

"I can live with it."

"Yes. Right. That's the spirit, Jim."

"And the furthermore?"

"What?"

"What's the *little more* to the experiment?"

"Oh, ah. We, that is, my, um, superiors, would like you to procreate."

Jim was stunned into speechlessness. What an absurd request, he thought, and what cheek.

"Impossible," he said at last.

"Why so?"

"Well, I have two wonderful children, I'm getting a little too old to raise any more, and, besides, Sharilyn has had her tubes tied, complications after Angie and all. It's impossible."

"Sharilyn's little malfunction can be brushed aside in a twinkling. She can be made quite ready. All we need is a willingness from you to proceed."

Jim thought hard. He tried to order his thoughts, squinting at the picnickers at nearby tables, at one toddler who was digging rancid chicken bones out of a bee-devilled trash container while his oblivious parents sat in miserable silence. The sun, directly overhead, burned with a dazzle which washed the scene of its edges. And Jim's heart opened to the child, to all the children. Yes, he thought, I could raise another.

"Okay, Mr. Shrive," Jim said finally. "I'll father again. But what do you hope to prove by this?"

"Nothing much, Jim. Just checking out the equipment so to speak. Oiling the infinite works, see. Don't you worry about that end. You'll hear no more from me. It will be as if none of this ever happened and you are free to live your happy and love-laden life, governed solely by your own will."

*

And this is the way it was.

Jim Cherry drank in his existence, day to day, with the same sort of tenderness and vigor he had been utilizing in this the second half of his life. He and Sharilyn made love, passionately and often, and, if she sensed a purpose behind the fervor, she mentioned it not. She only held on and reveled, grasping her Jim, her mate in the journey.

And it came to pass that Sharilyn woke one morning with a familiar nausea, a fluttering in her vitals which she remembered and knew for what it was. She was fearful. What type of ensorcelment was this? A false pregnancy to bait her, to reemphasize her inert apparati? She felt, initially, that something was wrong, something insidious, destined to foul up her contentment, her fresh, new life. Grit in the cream.

She didn't know how to broach the subject with Jim. But, one evening after bathing both children and seeing them off to sleep, she settled next to her husband and took a preliminary deep breath.

"What?" Jim said immediately.

"Honey," Sharilyn whispered, her voice hoarse with emotion, misgiving.

"Shar, Godsake, what's wrong?" Jim spoke now, quickly, afraid one of the children had a lump again (an early parenting panic).

"I'm p-p-pregnant," she sobbed.

Jim waited a beat, preparing his feigned astonishment.

"Jesus," he said, running a hand through his hair. It was a performance. "How. How could you be?"

"I don't know," Sharilyn said, now shaking with gulps of feeling. "I took the test though. It's positive. Positive."

"Ohmigod."

"I know."

"When did you suspect? I mean, had you missed a logo?"

"Period?"

"Of course."

"Yes. I mean, I guess. You know I haven't been that regular. I just figured it was something I didn't need to keep track of anymore. Oh, Jim. Should I be miserable?"

"Oh, Shar."

"I mean, I don't know. Is this something we can do?"

Jim appeared to think it over, studio-wrestling with the thorny predicament.

"Yes. Yes, Sharilyn, if you want to. I'm prepared to do it."

Sharilyn threw her arms around her foolishly grinning spouse and Jim beamed with the satisfaction of a dumb show well-executed. Sharilyn relaxed into her husband's determination and assurance, her life reconfiguring, crystallizing around her like a house of ice. It was all new, it was really all new.

As the months accumulated and the visits to the midwife became part of the routine again and the children adjusted to a different future, in which their parents' love was spread even thinner, like spider web, like Elastic Plastic, the Cherrys reconfirmed their abiding familial togetherness. They were quite a sight to see, and the neighbors whispered about what a model family they were as if reporting indiscretions. And it *was* practically shameful the way they radiated gratification, an unintentional happier-than-thou aura.

Sharilyn's water broke one Tuesday evening in November like the twanging of a single guitar string. Practiced in this now the Cherrys knew the signs, were comfortable with the amount of time they had, calmly called Katy to take the kids, called the midwife who assured them she would be there on time and would call ahead to the hospital and arrange the arrangements, grabbed their prepacked bag, and drove the 7.3 miles to St. Thomas Hospital.

And as prepared as they were, the birth, like all births, was concurrently a thing of magisterial beauty and a plunge into suprahuman pandemonium.

Babel, hysteria, benevolence. Those crowded moments, flashes of light, as if divine. The rush of faces and hands, and during all this Jim Cherry, outside of time, felt a clutching in his chest. The delivery room, the room of delivery. Deliver me, O Lord...

And during all this Jim Cherry felt the clutching in his chest, the flutter there, and was, in short, afraid. Afraid this was it, all he had left, these frenetic moments, his wife grim faced and clenched, the noisy mouths around him, swallowing up all air, all sense. He felt foreign to it, foreign to all of life, a specter, an uneasy presence.

But Jim Cherry did not die there. He did not. He survived to hold his wife the morning after and kiss her wrinkled brow and tell her how brave she was. Jim Cherry died two days later, in a Walgreens parking lot, where he had ventured on a mission for his expanding family. He drove out that evening for sanitary napkins for his sanguinolent wife, who bled the blood of life onto their full-sized bedsheets, who bled so that their son Chris could be born, could enter this sad old world with every prospect of a long and fruitful life.

And he died, Jim Cherry, quietly, in the front seat of his car, behind his steering wheel, in a Walgreens parking lot, his last sight an old man with a handful of fliers, begging, sad eyed, preaching to no one.

Jim Cherry lived long enough, though, to bring his new son home, his delicate little frame swaddled in hospital blankets. Jim Cherry lived long enough to unwrap the boy and marvel at his evanescent flesh, smell the sticky black meconium, like something infernal, in his first diaper, to rub the feathery little nubs on each shoulder blade where the child's inchoate wings poked through.

Jim felt those preliminary, aliform growths, and he thought about his life and its pied beauty, its embarrassment of riches, and he thought about Mr. Shrive, and the Otherworld, and the plan, and Jim Cherry saw it all whole, just for a moment and for the first time, and he thought that it was good.

Punk Band

Chuck calls me. It's been months.

"I've got a great idea," he says.

"Okay," I bat back.

"A punk band."

"That *is* a great idea," I say, facetiously. Chuck.

"What?"

"They've already thought of them."

"No, fuckhead, we start one."

"We can't play any, you know, musical instruments."

"Right," Chuck says in that overconfident way he has that is sometimes endearing and sometimes grating. "That's punk."

"Okay," I say.

"You sing," he thinks to add.

"I can't carry a tune in, what, a raku?"

"I don't know what that is, but, that's my point. You're our word guy. The poet of the obscene."

"Ah."

"I'm gonna play bass."

"Have you ever even seen a bass?"

"Sure. On TV."

"Right."

"Hey, Sid Vicious did it."

"Somehow I thought we'd get around to that."

"You're dubious, you mock."

"We're a little old for this."

"This is gonna keep us young. Out there. Cutting edge."

"Hey, I just flashed on a great name for the band."

"Yeah?"

"Jism."

"See, I knew you'd get aboard. Fucking Jeb, I told Whit. He'll get aboard."

"Whit is…"

"He wants to play drums. He's the only one with money enough to buy a set."

*

Our first practice was at Whit Whitaker's. I think this was because, once assembled, he was unsure if he could take his drum kit apart and put it together again.

Joining us was Larrivee on guitar. Larrivee is his last name but it's all he wants to be called. He actually knows how to play the guitar. And someone I didn't know on marimba, cowbell, and cardboard box, who called himself Norm du Plume. I'm sure this isn't his real name.

And, finally, Garland Draper, who is lovely. And that *is* her real name.

"Who's the woman?" I pulled Chuck aside.

"Garland Draper."

"I know her name. I heard her say her name. What does she play?"

"Nothing," Chuck says, in that way.

"Nothing."

"Well, she's going to add assorted vocalizings."

"Then I am not the singer. Thank God."

"You're the singer," Chuck says as if this is still obvious.

"And Garland…"

"Will add miscellaneous grunts and squeals and whistles and hums and backup. Wait till you hear her. She can do amazing things in her throat."

This is beginning to sound like quite an avant-garde group. Is this punk? I really have no idea.

"Just a quick jam to loosen up?" Larrivee asks.

"Great," Whit says from behind his colossal cymbals.

"How about "I Fought the Law," Larrivee asks.

"Great," Whit says.

"You know that?" Chuck asks me.

"I can't sing," I say.

"Right," he says.

"I know the words," I think to add.

"Great," says Whit.

Whit clicks his drumsticks together three times. I'm sure he saw this on TV.

Larrivee launches into a fluid guitar intro and Whit and Chuck stumble behind him. It sounds vaguely like "I Fought the Law." Norm du Plume is banging away on his marimba and cardboard box. The result is like a thunderstorm in the middle of the Beatles' dissolution. Raw. Like meat left on the sink overnight.

A marimba didn't seem right for a punk band—Norm said he found it at the dump—but, to his credit, Norm du Plume played a mean cardboard box.

I don't know where to jump in. Larrivee nods his head at me.

"Breaking rocks in the hot sun," I speak into the microphone. I'm standing back from it and leaning forward as if I expect it to strike like a cobra.

I speak a few more verses and suddenly Garland Draper is next to me saying something like "doodling-doo-doodling—ooo" into my mike. She smells like milk bath.

After about four chaotic minutes we stop.

"Great," says Whit.

*

I would have bet the farm that this experiment had about as much chance of succeeding as Nixon's skullduggery.

And, yet, after about two months we actually were starting to sound like a punk band. Or, what we thought punk bands sounded like.

I grew more comfortable in front of the mike and my spoken singing style was somewhere between Rex Harrison's and Frank Zappa's. Larrivee told me to put more grit into my voice. It worked.

And, with Larrivee's help, we began to forge our own songs, using my words as the lyrics we would gargle into the din.

My early attempts at songwriting were pitiful. But, I was making headway.

One afternoon Garland Draper appeared on my doorstep.

My girlfriend, Page, was away. She was almost always away. She was almost not my girlfriend.

"Larrivee said, maybe, I should help with the songwriting."

"Come in," I answered.

"Larrivee said since I was sort of the backup singer that maybe I should know more about the words."

This sounded better.

"Um, sure," I said. "You want a soda?"

"You got any tequila?" she hummed.

"Uh, no, no tequila. Do people keep tequila in their homes?"

I was honestly baffled.

"I don't know," she answered. "I don't."

This was an awkward conversation.

"You wanna see some of the lyrics I'm working on?"

"Yeah," she shrugged. She said everything as if it were a shrug.

I showed her about a dozen songs I was finished with or in the middle of. These included "Shark Snack," "For Kim Because it Went By So Fast," "Goddamned Past Full of Sex," "Jeopardous Heart," "Hogmagundy," "An Afternoon with Godard," "Helen Across Time," "Vertiginous Waves of Murmuring Need," and, what was to become our signature tune, "Sleep, Silence, Death."

"These are wonderful," Garland Draper said, looking up. Her eyes were the color of loam. She smelled like milk bath.

"Thanks," I said. "I have no idea how to write a song."

"Nonsense," she said. "You're our poet of the obscene."

Chuck.

*

It was startling to me when we actually started getting gigs. I felt foolish—I still feel foolish—using the word "gigs." Who was I kidding?

Our first public appearance was outdoors, in Overton Park, in an afternoon concert at the Shell, which also featured Neon Wheels and Tav Falco. How Chuck ever got us on this bill was beyond me. We opened. Neon Wheels and Tav Falco were waiting in the wings and, surprisingly, very kind to us naives. They helped us by telling us where to put our equipment and where to stand and how to use the microphone so that you didn't sound like a high school thespian. I was discomfited to be pointed out as the singer.

Of course, we had to take another name for the advertisements for this triple billing. Chuck came up with Ginger and the Minnow Crew. Garland was now called Ginger on stage. I hated Chuck's new name, so twee, so Chuck.

And we began what became a tradition. At the opening of every concert Chuck would intone, "Our real name is Jism, but they wouldn't let us put that on the posters."

This generally got a good laugh.

And we always began with "I Fought the Law." I admit this was a good choice. A rollicking good song and a statement of purpose. And Garland and I had formed a sort of intertwining singing/talking style that sounded weird and off-center and just right for the times.

We began playing around town. Small clubs, often at The Antenna, which was a hellhole and hence the center of punkdom in Memphis. Black Flag played there. I think REM did. We were still clumsy on stage but getting better.

One night at The Antenna we were in the middle of "Secretly All Women Are Named Suzie," an original that started out as "The Agoraphobic's Pandiculations," but through alchemy and tired, late-hour rehearsals became one of our better songs. There was a buzz in the crowd. Alex Chilton was in attendance.

And, suddenly, I saw him, off to the left of the stage, almost in shadow, a small, wiry man, arms crossed, appraising us. Garland was oblivious and I sure didn't want to clue her in. I was as nervous as Macbeth before the ghost of Banquo.

I botched some of the lyrics, fluffed a whole verse, repeated another. Instead of "She's off her rock, I got a tip about those kind of women," I sang, "She's off like a rocket, tipped, a kind woman." Garland thought I was ad-libbing, scatting to my own disheveled lyrics. She began to grunt and howl with renewed enthusiasm. Her hand went to my lower back as she leaned into the mike; she almost caressed my right buttock.

Really, most of my earnestly wrought lyrics were lost in the pandemonium of Whit's pounding and Norm's boxing. Still, it made me panicky and I wanted to impress Garland, still. She smelled like milk bath and sweat.

Her soft caress helped me through. A sort of symbiosis was forming between us.

We finished the number. We counted ten and launched into "Blunge." When I stole a glance at where Alex Chilton had been he was gone, like smoke. Had he really been there, I thought. Somehow we made it through our set.

And, afterward, we were all at the back, near the bar, near the frightening hall which seemed to be an entranceway to

Gehenna but only led to the bathrooms. On it was written every kind of obscenity. Love is dead.

Suddenly, Mr. Chilton was standing next to me. I was a good head taller than him. Or a bad head.

I smiled a tight smile, almost an apology.

"You guys kick ass," he said, simply.

Whit whispered, "Great."

Chuck stumbled over the feet around him to reach us.

"Alex," he said, as if they were old compadres. "Chuck Kom."

They shook hands. Alex Chilton looked like he was almost asleep.

"We're looking for studio time," Chuck said, overly anxious. I felt for him. Fucking Chuck.

The stillness of a sepulcher surrounded us. I turned to take a swig of my beer before remembering I hadn't ordered one, nor did I drink beer.

Garland slipped her arm through mine.

"Gimme your number. I'll call you," Alex Chilton said.

We were sanctified. We were validated.

*

You know a lot of the rest, if you listen to this kind of cacophony. We recorded our first album at Ardent, with Alex Chilton producing. "Suck it Up," by Chism (our compromise), became something of a local cause célèbre and, nationally, actually charted somewhere in the high 90's.

This was before compact discs. Like many musicians in our chosen genre we would have eschewed the new and committed solely to vinyl, because we were pure, but it wasn't an issue until later. It is only through the love and persistence of some of our supporters (thanks always, Alex, Jim) that our work now exists on CD.

Here is the song list from "Suck it Up," for those who never picked up a copy:

Side One:
Helen Across Time
The Agoraphobic's Pandiculations
Hogmagundy
A Party in Diddy-Wah-Diddy
For Kim Because it Went By So Fast
Sleep, Silence, Death

Side Two:
Blunge
A Day of Rue
It'll Kill Me If it Doesn't Kill You First
Cicisbeo
Shlomo in Love
Child
Dakini Blues
and, hidden, uncredited on the LP but listed on the subsequent CD, our bombs-bursting-in-air version of "I Fought the Law"

That was our first studio effort. In retrospect it's not a bad endeavor. It has a certain *energy* to it, missing perhaps on our later LPs. I still pull it out occasionally and give it a listen. It makes me smile to hear that cardboard percussion or

Larrivee's smooth-as-a-river guitar. Even Chuck's ridiculous thumping on bass guitar has an élan that more-polished groups missed. But, it makes me cry to hear Garland's voice, as sinuous as a serpent, as smoky as night-swollen mushrooms.

My own "singing" still embarrasses me: like the shouting of a backstay in a gale, as Kipling said.

From there it was more live playing, more money, and the offer of a second record deal. The good folks at Ardent treated us like rock stars and damned if we didn't try to act like we were. Bless our hearts.

Page left me somewhere between our first and second albums. I hardly noticed.

Our second album, "Vertiginous Waves of Murmuring Need," should have collapsed under the weight of its pretentious title. But this was 1979 and such affectations were not only accepted, they were rewarded.

Alex didn't produce this one. It is listed as "Produced by Chism, Engineered by John Kilzer," but, really, without John we would have been whistling in the wind. John also contributed one track to the album, the beautiful "Figs," on which Garland took her only solo singing credit. She should have fronted the band. I felt that then and I sure as hell feel it now.

Garland.

Even the list of songs on our sophomore album seems to me now precious, affected, and weighted with self-importance. From the opening "Story of Chism" to the closing "Goddamned Past Full of Sex," the whole thing is wordy, silly, fraught with a "look at me" sensibility. In a way, given the posturing of the time it was recorded, it is a perfect album. The 80's were fixing to implode the whole punk movement and we stood at the cusp of that collapse. Forgive us. Pity us.

Hell, we made a lot of money. Where is it now?

We made one more album, in 1981, the forgettable "Vanity's Sister." It was a single long track and features the worst writing I have ever done in my life. I still like a line here and there:

"In Niagara Falls once I slept with a rock star's girlfriend's sister. I felt the great tear of that overflow underneath me, even as her hand reached down for something still and central."

But such concreteness was, for the most part, missing from that forty-eight-minute exercise in self-indulgence. It should be said that Chuck's departure from the band right before recording hurt our group-gestalt, but the addition of Renny White on bass was a real plus. What could we have done if we had stayed together? Here's my ideal line-up: Larrivee, Whit (yes, his drumming became more than competent, it became *distinctive*), Renny White, and the lovely Garland Draper on vocals. And, humbly, me in the murky dimness, listed only as "lyricist." Procol Harum got away with it.

What dulcet sounds could that group have accomplished? One can only speculate.

And, here's the wrap-up, like at the end of the movie where they tell you what happened to each character.

I turned my attention to writing full time, produced one novel, the experimental *Talk: A Novel in Dialogue*. It sank like a lark falling suddenly to earth. I got a job in a bookstore, where I am today, and where I am known as Jeb, the guy who writes wobbly poetry that appears in literary rags with readerships in the single digits.

Whit Whitaker drummed with The Elastic Jug Stompers for a while and when they disbanded, so to speak, he began teaching drum lessons out of his home. He married a sweet and patient woman named Sharilyn Hover. She used to sing with Dick Delisi's band but is now a nurse.

Norm du Plume, whoever he was, disappeared. Someone said he ran guns to the Sandinistas. I never heard anything else from or about him.

Larrivee, you know, plays with Taint, whose astronomical success is long running and deserved. They seem unassailable and can be seen on MTV and VH1 as regularly as back fence cats.

Chuck sells cars out on Covington Pike. Fucking Chuck.

And Garland, whom I miss with an ache like "the day let suddenly on sick eyes," also hit it big as a solo artist in the countrypolitan genre. Her appearances with Nanci Griffith and her platinum album, "Glimmerless," have established her as one of the most formidable artists in the nineties. She married Tony Jungklas, who played with Emmylou Harris. She may be the only woman I ever loved.

Though I never touched her.

Though I never said a single romantic word to her.

I wrote her one song, a song no one will ever sing: "Garland Draper in the Morning."

She smelled, listeners, like milk bath.

The Door

"Whatever hour you woke there was a door shutting."

—Virginia Woolf, "A Haunted House"

James Royce did not like it when his parents left him alone. Anywhere, at any time. Being sent to his room was especially galling to the ten-year-old because he liked nothing better than being in the middle of family doings. He resented his parents when they went out for the evening and left him with his older brother, Norm. And now that Norm was dating and going out on his own, James often felt left out. It was maddening and it was disorienting.

He never wanted to miss anything—even bedtime was difficult for him. He could hear the low-level burble of the TV from his room off the hallway. He could hear his mother occasionally making comment, something about "Mrs.

Pewitt," something about the church. He strained to hear—he had to know everything. Life was going on all around him.

Therefore, when he sat in the parlor—the overly decorated front room the Royces referred to as the parlor—he could feel the loneliness seep into his very bones. It made his limbs heavy. It made moving around difficult. He cursed the family for leaving—even though Norm was only in his own bedroom, down the hall, with the door closed and weird, Indian music leaking out of it.

James sat on the piano bench and studied the room. He had memorized its every contour, its minutia, like he had memorized the wallpaper at the dentist's office, which depicted a sylvan scene of indeterminate time, a swirling, off-green representation of a world that, really, never existed. The parlor was dark, the drapes of a heavy synthetic material that blocked nearly all light. They drained the room. The furniture seemed made of the same opaque substance, as if the whole room was webby, or an undersea city like Atlantis. James thought about being underwater, the pressure on every square inch of you, the suffocating weight.

And as he mused on things dim and melancholy and shadowy, a slight movement to his left disturbed his peripheral attention. He slowly turned his head toward the disturbance, if disturbance it was. His eye fell on the closet door. James measured it. It had opened itself, he thought. While he was sitting there the door had opened—just that. It was now slightly ajar; an inhospitable sliver of darkness now appeared between door and jamb.

A shiver went through James. Why would a door suddenly open? He did not like thinking about it. The dark sliver drew him. It was an obdurate black—a black that swallowed light, swallowed sight. James had to get out of the room—that's what he knew. He had to get out but his limbs felt so exhausted. Could he run, or would it be like the dream where his legs would not move, as if clothed in concrete?

He looked at the door that led to the hallway and then to Norm's room. He could make it. He could just make it.

He rose like an automaton and moved quietly out of the room. He could hear Norm's music. Familiarity flooded him. He was safe for now.

*

"There's something creepy about the front parlor," James tried at breakfast the next day. His father snorted under his mustache.

"James," was all he said, a one-word disruption of his newspaper perusal.

James' mother was more accommodating.

"What's creepy about the parlor, dear?" she asked, placing cinnamon toast on the table.

"I think there's—uh—something in there," James said. "Sort of."

"Sort of in there?" his mother asked.

"I mean, the door in there—" James stopped himself. A door opening itself is not exactly the most fearful thing in the mind of adults. James recognized this now.

"Nevermind," he said.

"Just stay out of there then," his mother smiled at him.

"Squirt" was Norm's only addendum.

*

A few days went by. A few days of kickball and curb-sitting and sweat and mosquitoes. A few days of the Dorich brothers and their athleticism and guns. Summer was its usual under-the-surface self, voices that whisper, mumble, and intimate an adventure that is just beyond reach, one that stays just beyond reach. Summer promised much and delivered in percentages.

So it was that one afternoon James was alone in the house—his mother standing near the backyard fence, swapping privations with Mrs. Pewitt.

The house ticked as beams pandiculated. A fug fell over the entire home—born of heat and air that seemed weighted with something other than humidity, an indolence, an oppression. The parlor called to James—it petitioned something base and basic to human curiosity, a desire to see the worst, to experience the dreadful, and then to measure one's self.

James entered the room as if he were entering church, a church filled with strangers who worshipped strangeness. He left the joining door open—it allowed a weak, cloying light to waft in and mingle with the murk like a poor solution. James shuffled his feet, a tentativeness that addressed the parlor's influence.

He returned to the piano bench. Everything seemed the same as on his previous visit. He could hear the air conditioner make its mechanical sleep sounds, a machine laboring against the world's seriousness. James imagined that in its susurration he could perceive the voices of drowned men, of mermen and Triton's gulag.

Somewhere in the distance a lawnmower started up, a razory buzz. And underneath it, perhaps, his mother's bright chatter.

James had not looked at the door. Now, as confidence leeched into him, he slowly turned toward it. It was closed.

In his mind he could see the inside of the closet. It held seasonal things—winter things—and hence was all but forgotten in the summer, just as winter's hardships were. James could see his coat, too thick for comfort, his rubbers, the sled against the back wall, held in place by heavy outerwear hanging on the cross rod.

Then he saw it happen as if his attention were causing it. The door opened with a smart *click*. The same one inch of darkness presented itself. James could only stare. It opened— *for him*. The door knew he was there. It opened *because* he was looking at it. What did it want?

James looked quickly to the outer door, making sure his egress would be unimpeded. The outer door was closed. James knew he had left it open.

Now, panic rose in him like an ague. He sprang from the bench, grabbed frantically at the outer door, his small hand glancing off the polished doorknob, until in his fumbling he was able to open it. He caromed off the walls in the hall, his breath coming in painful swallows, and he all but bowled over his mother coming inside just then, clothespins still in her mouth.

"James," she spat a pin into her palm. "What in the world?"

*

Later, James lay on his bed with a washcloth over his forehead. He had gotten overheated, his mother said, all corrective and utility. And she comforted him with a universal palliative.

"Don't carry on so," she admonished.

James was willing to believe that he had just been carrying on. Once returned to the known world, once more among family members and adult reason, his misadventure in the parlor seemed harebrained, at best. Afraid of a door? Ridiculous.

Later, in Norm's room, James lay on the bottom bunk and spoke to the mattress above him as if it were his father confessor. Norm lay on the top bunk leafing through a *Mad Magazine*, only half-listening to his moon-stricken little brother.

"There are things in the world, in the ordinary world, that when you look at them too closely, you know, become creepy. Ordinary things. You ever have that happen?" James tried to keep the whine out of his voice.

"Uh huh," Norm said, his concentration lost on the back-page fold.

"Really?" James said. "You know what I mean?"

"Mean about what?" Norm said, returning, slowly.

"Things. Things you are familiar with. You look at them and they...*change*."

"What are you on about?" Norm said, now all big-brotherly.

"The door in the parlor." There. He'd said it.

"What about it? You're scared of the door in the parlor?"

"See..."

"Squirt, c'mon. You want to see me take that door in hand? Is that what you want? You know what—I'll *open* it. Whad' ya say?"

This was the kind of action he counted on Norm for. This was taking the bull by the horns. Norm would save him from his inner demons.

*

Someone had pulled the heavy curtains back in the parlor. A buttery shard of light fell on the floor, unredeemed. The room quivered in the gloam.

Norm looked it over quickly and then turned to his younger brother. His expression said, I don't get it.

Norm walked to the closet door and yanked it open. Inside were the coats and toys and boxed games and dusty effluvia of seasons past. Nothing seemed menacing or inappropriate or even out of place. Norm scanned the interior.

"Nothing here, Squirt, unless you find old sleds frightening."

James wanted to say, it's not what's in there, it's the door itself. It has cognition. It *knows* when James is in the room. He didn't know what he wanted to say—he simply couldn't explain the feeling that came over him when the door opened.

"That's okay," James said, investing his speech with a lightness that he did not feel. "It'll be okay."

*

Days went by, the measured dog days of summer. James did not return to the parlor. He spent his time in front of the television, or reading Hardy Boys, or playing at anarchy with the Dorich boys. They rifled construction sites for their discarded gold. They stole *Playboys* from the 7/11. They undressed in empty houses to marvel at the differences in their private parts. Once they tormented a bat that had inexplicably flown into the sidewalk—a bat in daylight was a thing *other.*

The sun was relentless, a blazing voice in the sky that rendered each day a heated trance. The boys sat on curbs and talked about forbidden things. They pelted passing cars with ice cubes. They sailed stick boats down swollen gutter drains. Everything seemed simple, predestined.

Norm came and went, finding his way into young girls' hearts. He brought home a stream of varying models of young womanhood, as if his only delight was in their dissimilarity, or as if they were samples to be tried and either abandoned or venerated. They all seemed to be named Susie or Laurie. They all smiled, their brilliant teeth an exemplar of money and superior breeding. They all wore shirts that clung to their burgeoning breasts like good packaging. And they all seemed to worship Norm, holding onto his arm, or touching him when they spoke, or laughing at everything he said. Norm drifted through this time an observer of his own life, an objective explorer. Norm did not recognize that this was a golden time because we do not, none of us. James thought his brother just shy of a god.

James' parents, at this time, also seemed to drift. But their drifting was of a different quality. They were adults who had achieved what they set out to achieve. And now they wanted nothing more than to watch it happen around them, in flow, a life like a garden. They smiled at their children, were proud of them, trusted that their lives were taking shape and form. James felt calmer in their presence. He almost forgot about the door in the parlor.

But almost is not creed. It is neither meal nor balm. Almost is a place of ghosts and recalcitrant waft.

James knew he would return to the parlor and he only half-believed that the days since he'd been there, the days of heat and distraction, had inured him, had fashioned around him a protective crust.

*

Still, James made no conscious decision to return. One day, a day of liquid hours and empty reverie, James found himself standing on the threshold of the parlor. Somewhere his mother was singing to herself, a song about Joan of Arc. James could just hear her voice, as if from afar, as if she were singing on a radio tuned low. James stood outside the room and looked at it for a long time. How could something so familiar—something owned by his family, a part of his life, a part of him—seem so eerie, so outside of workaday existence? It was like when James found himself peering at the back of his hand as it lay lifeless on the table before him. He didn't recognize it—the russet hair on his knuckles, the knob of joints—and a queer feeling came over him. It was attached to him, yet foreign.

Now, James stepped into the parlor. There was a muffled pucker in sound, similar to a pressure drop. James worked his jaw as if the relief were there. He sat on the piano bench, his back to the door. His fingers picked out "Michael, Row the Boat Ashore," a small, desultory reverberation, like rain on tarpaper.

He craned his head toward the closet. Nothing seemed amiss. It was the door Norm had opened so casually, the very same door. Behind it were winter belongings, that was all.

James turned his body round. He forced himself to hold his gaze on the door. The door appeared to respire, a slight expansion like a current of air brings about. Yet, on this day, there was nothing fearful in its symmetry, its outline, its very *doorness*. James felt silly—all those days he had spent worrying over something his imagination had fomented. Really, he was a moony child, a beetlehead.

Just then it happened again. The door cracked. The black nothingness that it presented was the black nothingness that James feared most. Just that—a single, solid band of black that obliterated light, reason, hope. There rose in James a dread as dire as death, as foul as corruption. Tears welled in him, a sinister crapulence.

James quickly turned toward the exit—his hope—and the door was again closed. Had he left it open? His mind was jumbled. He turned back toward the blackness. Did he hear a whisper, a sound like the night makes? Was it his name? No, this was fancy—of course it was. James knew better than to believe that inanimate things doomed him. The world is neither stacked for nor against you, his father said.

Yet, the closet seemed to have a connection to him. What was this connection? What did it portend?

James stood, a sleepwalker. He moved toward the closet. Was it bravery? Was it damned curiosity? He was drawn closer.

Now, as he stood within a few feet of the opening, he was sure it was breathing, murmuring, making sounds of entreaty. James' body felt bottom-heavy, his legs weighted attachments. His hand went to the knob.

The doorknob was cold, as cold as a graveyard stone. James pulled the door toward him—it moved so easily, soundlessly, naturally. The door was as weightless as cloud. It felt right to James, and a calm entered him.

James stood and looked into the darkness before him. It was a void, an abyss of impenetrable blackness. Its end was time's end, its boundaries that of the soul's limits. James felt oddly penitent yet untainted before it. He felt as if he could stay there forever, on the threshold of something larger than himself. He knew that what faced him beckoned, as each day the time you have left beckons, a skeleton's curled finger, a faith.

James moved forward, his fingertips numb. His foot felt for something solid, but, in the end, it didn't matter. He continued to move forward.

*

Months later, James' mother would still not get out of bed. James' father put his hand to his wife's brow and felt the dew there. Her eyes were vacant, scorched earth.

"Today," he said, hopefully. His words dropped into a crack in the world.

He went to work anyway, because one does. Because it's eventually expected.

Norm began dating a Laurie steadily, their bond something like the middle of the fairy tale, before the part where recompense comes. Laurie had not yet pricked her finger; Norm had not yet wounded his thigh.

And the Royces' house, where they lived and loved and wept and bled and cried and died and were reborn over and over, grew unnaturally still, as if it knew something, something beyond telling. The house was hushed now, as deeply sunk in mystery as a dream ship, and an ambiguity was present, like the ineffable matter that surely bonds one human being to another.

Blunge

"The false or substituted bride is one of the most widespread of all folktale motifs."

—Funk & Wagnalls Standard Dictionary of Folklore, Mythology, and Legend

I never noticed before. My wife is left-handed. This gives me pause as I stand in the doorway, a mixer dripping with cake batter in my hand. She's always been so loving, with the kids and all.

On TV there is a nature show, the kind of thing she likes, one predator on top of another. I watch her watch for a few minutes. One drip falls from my blades and, in slow motion, careens floorward. It lands and there is that frozen moment, an explosion.

Somewhere in the farthest corners of the house I can hear the muffled sounds of our children, lost in their own worlds, lost to us.

My wife turns toward me and sees me standing there. The terror in her face is worth the forfeited time, the mess. I return to the kitchen, a different man. I am armed now. There will be no more secrets, no more surprises from here on out, from the middle of my life till the final reconsideration.

Supermarket

> "The A&P is a supermarket, a higher exchange, an inexhaustible reservoir, a place so complete it can embrace its own contradictions: it is both abattoir and garden, sacrifice and harvest, death and life."
>
> —James P. Carse, from *Breakfast at the Victory*

Robert Caldwell was a man like a lot of us, who did not enjoy random human encounters, who, indeed, avoided them at all costs. He did not mesh well with the workaday world, or, at least, he believed he did not. And this is the same thing.

On bad days the smallest task was beyond him. He dodged the duties which require confrontations with official servants of the public good: arguing traffic tickets, getting the car inspected, taking out a loan. Normally, his wife, Gayla, accomplished these assignments for him. When they bought their house, it was painful for Robert to meet with the real estate agent (even though she was a friend), and even more painful when they had to close and meet with a lawyer.

In the circle of his friends Robert was known as an affable, pleasant man, one given to jokes and reassuring pats on the back. So, he was high functioning, to use a fancy word, in his day-to-day life, a manager of a small, independent movie theater, who was known in the narrow circle of midtown Memphis for his good taste and knowledge of films. Not a public figure, certainly, but, in his particular artistic domain, he had a reputation.

Such are the mysteries of the human heart that such a dichotomy exists. The chasm between public persona and private sensitivity is wide, is extraordinary. But, there's nothing overridingly unconventional about Robert Caldwell; he's no better or worse off than the majority of men, who, as Thoreau said, lead lives of quiet desperation.

Enough said, then. One Sunday morning Robert Caldwell went to the grocery store, the same grocery store he had been going to for the last ten years, with no foreboding, a man on a simple errand, out for his weekly food run.

There was no trepidation attached to this particular visit. It was routine, practiced. Robert did it every week with no more thought than he used to sign the monthly mortgage bill. He had a list. He methodically checked items off his list as he located them in the store. He located items in the store with little or no searching, due to his familiarity with this specific grocery store. And, if the store personnel did not know Robert Caldwell, it was due to the volume of traffic they encountered in their necessarily very public jobs, or due to Robert's regular good looks, neither overly handsome nor remarkably bad looking.

Robert wheeled his crippled cart deliberately down one aisle and up another, never skipping one, not even the Diaper/Pet

Food/ Hardware aisle, though the Caldwells had neither child nor animal nor were particularly inclined to do their own repairs, however minor. Still, aisle 11 was part of the route, the prescribed circuit.

Today the stockboys seemed lethargic, surly, as if some exotic flu had overtaken them all. Robert reached in front of one young man clad in excessively baggy jeans and required white apron, in the produce aisle, to squeeze a cantaloupe, and the boy's expression reminded Robert of one of the undead. Robert moved on.

While scrutinizing the fish selection Robert paused to catch the tune the muzak was cloning. It was Dylan's "Ballad of a Thin Man," an odd choice for a syrupy string arrangement. Robert smiled a bemused smile at the absurdity of modern existence.

As Robert neared the checkout his heart did a brief tattoo, nothing major, a slight dipping in its accentuation. The open cashier suddenly before him, her aisle as free of business as a cloudless sky, he found a tad severe, a large, black woman who perpetually scowled. Robert, as we know, was not the type to engage in small talk anyway, but this woman was menacing in her every movement; she had a body language which whispered intimidation. "Clairice" her name tag read, a most unlikely moniker. Robert regularly avoided her aisle.

Her blackness had nothing to do with Robert's fear. He was satisfied in his own heart that this was so. He did not fear other cultures—at least, no more than he feared his own. It had more to do with her size, her furrowed brow, her habit of sliding products across her scanner with a rapid right-to-left movement, as if she were slinging mucus from her spread fingers. A motion of disgust, of an unwillingness to work with the objects of the world, an antipathy for things.

Clairice looked up and took in Robert's hesitation at the mouth of her pathway, the territory she policed. Her ebony face was a mask of unfeeling; her stillness spoke volumes. It said *come on, ofay, move your ass.*

Robert smiled a tight little smile and pushed his cart forward a tad too quickly. It did not clear the ridge over which it was supposed to rest, but shocked him with a dull encounter that shook his teeth. Clairice registered no emotion and, instead, began to drag items across the computerized eye of her glass countertop. Her substantial hands worked with world-weary accuracy. Robert noticed that each nail on each finger had been painted a sky blue and garnished with a black ace of spades.

Robert prepared his checkbook and pen, already writing in the name of the store and signing his name. No good to keep the customers behind him waiting—he was considerate. He waited patiently for the foodstuffs to pass one by one over the scanner.

Then it happened. The Red Baron frozen pizzas, clearly marked with a sale tag on their shelf, at 2 for $6.00, rang in at $3.99 each. Robert paused and then cleared his throat. Clairice rested not, the items flying now, a blur of colored cardboard packaging. Robert tried another preparatory cough, one which would arrest any ordinary retail clerk, one which, in all societies, signaled the beginning of an interruption, the cessation of all previous activity for the coming on of speech.

"I'm sorry," Robert now had to toss out.

Clairice lifted her large, round, expressionless face.

"Those pizzas," Robert nodded toward his groceries, already bagged by the efficient young man at the end of the counter.

"Yeah," Clairice intoned.

"I think they rang up wrong."

Clairice breathed out a sigh which carried historical significance.

The young bagger stuck his face over the bags, his sleepy eyes searching out miscreants. He reached down, like a young Arthur, and pulled the two pizza boxes back out into the swirling air.

"They're on sale," Robert said, pleasantly.

"Uh huh," Clairice said, giving the receipt a perfunctory perusal.

"I think they're 2 for 6," Robert said, trying to sound breezy, trying to sound as if he were tapped into stockboy lingo. "They're on sale," he repeated, unnecessarily.

"You wanna go back and look again?" Clairice deadpanned.

"Uh," Robert hesitated and in that moment of hesitation lost whatever power he had held up to that point.

Clairice bent her head back to her task and the food began again gliding over the scanner. She was impervious, regal.

Robert felt the gall rise in his throat. He felt the beat of his heart quicken. Injustice was a heady tonic and it bubbled now in Robert's white, middle-class veins.

"You check it," Robert said, with perhaps a little more heat than intended, his voice breaking on the penultimate syllable. "Or him," Robert threw in, tossing his head in the silent stockboy's direction.

Clairice did a slow burn. Her voice, when it finally emerged from her ancient mask, was measured and sure.

"That sale over," was what she said.

But Robert had come too far now. He stood on the podium of truth and his gaze was austere, his jaw firm.

"You must honor the sign," he said, his voice gaining in timbre and vitality.

Clairice stood stock-still for one moment only. And then she managed something truly impressive. She smiled, an overly large, lopsided smile.

"Fuck you, Charlie," she said under her breath, and bent inexorably to the task at hand. She slid the remaining items over the center of her private principality and spoke with tried and tired regularity.

"$98.69," Clairice said.

Robert stared at his nemesis with a stony resolve. There was a clarity to him now. He stood defined against the background of mass commercialism, a warrior. Around his tunnel vision was a mist of delineation, simplifying his certitude. His heart beat a steady and inspiring cadence, the drumming of what is right. He would not falter now.

"I need to see your supervisor," he said, and then added with a dash of impropriety, "Clairice."

The on-duty supervisor that day was Delray Pervus, a gangly youth of nineteen who looked fifteen, even though what was once a bad case of acne had now been diminished to a bad case of pitted scars. Delray was summoned to register 6 over the store loudspeaker and he approached the register area with a smirky, pursed grin affixed to the center of his cicatricial cheeks.

"Whatsa problem here," he leaked from his rident visage.

Clairice jerked a thumb toward Robert, who was reduced to a momentary sticky wicket, a speed bump in the inconversable clerk's busy day.

Robert cleared his already clear throat and said, reasonably, "We had a disagreement over an item's price and she became very rude."

"A disagreement?" the supervisor simpered.

"You rude," Clairice proclaimed, succinctly.

"Well, that's not important. She swore at me," Robert said.

"The disagreement may be important, sir. Our prices are fair and firm," Delray spoke, the company line ready on his tongue.

"Yes, yes," Robert said, impatiently. "The point is she was rude to me. She swore at me."

"What did she say?"

Robert hesitated a crucial second.

"She said, 'Fuck you.'"

"I dint," Clairice said.

"Hmm," Delray said, ruminative hand on chin.

"Look," Robert began.

"I think we'll have to refer this to downstairs," Delray pronounced.

Robert saw Clairice register a moment of surprise, a slight widening of the eyes, which betrayed—what? Robert looked awkwardly from Delray to Clairice. Maybe this was getting a little out of hand.

"Follow me," Delray Pervus said and set off down the Pasta/Sauces/Spices aisle with military determination.

Robert bumbled along after him, feeling foolish, as if he were following a teacher to the principal's office.

"Wait," he said, weakly, toward the rapidly moving back of the floor supervisor.

Delray disappeared through one-half of a pair of swinging doors beside the meat counter and Robert just caught the door on the backswing and toddled after. The cinder-block corridor was dark and damp and smelled of blood and sweat. To his right he flashed by a heavyset butcher, whose apron wore the imprint of a life of slaughter. Robert may have seen a large, ensanguined cleaver in the meaty hand at the butcher's side, or he may have imagined it.

The slender supervisor stepped off to his left at the end of the corridor and when Robert caught up he almost fell headfirst down a steep embankment of concrete stairs. He righted himself on the narrow walls of the passageway and saw Delray vanish behind a door at the foot of the stairway.

Through that door and down another long concrete-block passageway to another flight of cold, hard stairs, Robert felt as if he were descending into the Earth. It was cold and unforgiving, hard like he imagined prison. He hurdled on, trying to catch the descending supervisor's attention. He wanted to call the whole thing off; he wanted to go home.

Eventually Robert emerged through another white, metallic door into a room lit with a thousand lamps. After the murk of the halls the room was an assault on the eyes, the bright white like the blankness after death. Robert gasped and squeezed a hand over his pained peepers.

When he could see again he found himself in an anteroom, such as one finds in an ER, a sterile place of waiting. Delray Pervus was right at his side.

"If you'll just wait here," he intoned.

Robert raised a jaded hand.

"I think this is a bit much," he began.

Delray Pervus seemed offended.

"How so?" he inquired.

"Well, I mean," Robert grabbled. "I guess, it's only a few cents..."

Delray Pervus seemed to gather himself like a diva about to solo. His moony face squinched into a twisted mask.

"How dare you!"

"What?" Robert returned.

"You impugn our integrity, you insult our clerk, and now you wanna just go home and put your feet up."

Robert's sense of injustice was newly inflamed. His ire went beyond the spiny toad immediately before him: it took in the room, the store, the cold-blooded, uncaring planet.

"Okay, dammit, let's do it all, let's see it through to the end, let's just see the head honcho, let's get this straightened out. Maybe someone around here has some sense about how to treat a customer. Let's go—let's see your superior!" Robert fairly spat out.

Delray Pervus grew calmer in the face of Robert's outburst. He seemed to say, Now I know what I'm dealing with.

"Sit there," he said, like a prim schoolmaster, pointing his bony hand at a row of industrial chairs. He turned on his heel and once again was gone behind a forbidding door.

Robert dropped onto one of the hard cushions of the chairs and expelled a pent-up breath. Rage rattled in his chest; he found himself wringing his hands like some bad actor's imitation of Uriah Heep. He ran a sweaty palm over his hair.

A long time passed. His palms had dried. Robert began to suspect he had been abandoned. He stood and stepped toward the door and tentatively reached a hand for the knob. As if he were being watched the door sprung open right underneath his outstretched reach, freezing Robert in an embarrassing posture.

Delray Pervus stood on the other side, the picture of grim foreboding. There was something funereal about his pose, upright and somber, as if he were welcoming another sinner into hell.

"Down the hall, to the left," he said.

Robert started to say something, something slightly apologetic, peace-offering.

Delray raised an attenuated hand.

"Down the hall, to the left," he repeated.

Robert gathered his uneasy dignity and sidestepped past the ghastly supervisor and walked slowly down the hall.

At the end, on the left, was another door. This one, however, was wooden, warm, painted a forest green. It was like a door in a home, welcoming and friendly. Robert felt suddenly better. He didn't know whether to knock or just walk in. He settled for a light rap as he opened the door.

"Hi," he said, with as benevolent a grin as he could muster. He faced a desk the size of a battleship, as devoid of clutter as an airport tarmac; not even a phone marred its perfect, black surface. The only items resting on the desktop were the muscular hands of the store's manager. These hands drew Robert's attention: they were lightly coated with thin black hair and the interlaced fingers exuded a strength Robert could only admire, a strength which *ruled*.

Gradually Robert took in the rest of the individual before him, who seemed content to sit quietly while Robert made his assessments. The face above the exquisitely cut suit was the face of a devil, if one can conceive of the devil as movie-star handsome. There was something of the young Robert De Niro about him, something equally princely and evil. Then, as if a conjuring act had been achieved before his wondering eyes, Robert recognized his ghastly mistake. This was not a handsome man sitting before him in stately silence, but a woman, a woman in a business suit, with hair slicked back from her well-defined face with cunning severity. It was a face to be reckoned with, a beatific appearance; it was Oz. As Robert made the adjustment the face cracked ever so slightly with what Robert eventually realized was a smile. She smiled at the dawning of intelligence in Robert's countenance, and at Robert's smallness.

Robert crept forward in slow motion and took the chair in front of the desk as if it had been offered. He could not speak and waited only to be told what to do, crawl away, kiss her shoes, prostrate himself before the store's *maya*. This was not a mere grocery store he was dealing with, he realized, but a power, a presence, a principality ruled by empirism, judiciousness, love. He was nothing before it. He was less than nothing.

Finally the beautiful face opened and spoke.

"What is your name?" she asked, as if she were picking him up in a bar.

"Robert," Robert said. "Robert Caldwell."

She seemed to think about this.

Maybe he was wrong. Maybe Robert Caldwell was known to her and he was not him.

"You have insulted our clerk, I understand, Mr. Caldwell?"

"Well, no," Robert began. "That is, it was I, me, I who was insulted. Your clerk swore at me."

"That is not what she says," came the answer.

Was it possible this preeminence had already spoken to all available parties, had already called all the witnesses, had adjudicated and found him blameworthy?

"Well," Robert said again. "I merely questioned a price on some frozen pizzas and she..." Robert trailed off. "It sounds kind of silly now," he added.

"Is it silly?"

"I mean, it's just some crummy pizzas—"

"You're dissatisfied with our pizzas?"

"No," Robert said quickly. "No. I mean, it's not as important as all this."

"All what, Mr. Caldwell?"

"This folderol," Robert said, grandly.

She thought for a moment more.

"I'm quite at a loss what to do with you, Mr. Caldwell," she said with some stress.

Robert felt a tingling along the base of his neck.

The manager slowly rose from behind the desk, uncoiling her body like a constrictor. She moved from behind her judge's bench and Robert turned in his chair toward her. She moved as if she were an automaton, her feet seemingly rolling across the carpeted floor. As she emerged from behind her monstrous desk Robert comprehended her full majesty. She wore a short skirt with her suit jacket and her legs were strong and lithe, unstockinged they shone with a rosy glare. She stood next to his chair and her large, fulsome body exuded an animal musk. Despite his fear Robert felt a stiffening in his trousers, inappropriate as an erection on the gallows.

She turned Robert toward her and he realized for the first time that his chair was on wheels. She stood almost astride him, her legs slightly parted and her powerful thighs on each side of his. She took his face in her warm, moist hands and lifted his gaze upward. She bent to look closely into his eyes and Robert saw revealed underneath her suit coat and lacy shirt the swell of life, two onerous mammaries.

"So, Robert Caldwell," she said, peering into his very soul, her hands moving gently on his cheeks.

The air was full of static. Robert was warmed by her proximity.

"I'm sorry," she said after a moment. "I'm not going to be able to let you go."

Robert wasn't sure he had heard her. He was muddled, sweating. His ears seemed to be filled with a low-range rumble as of some incessant machine deep in the bowels of the store. He was afraid, aroused—save for the blood flow to his genitals he could not feel his body. He was sure at any moment she would laugh and they would exchange companionable touches and it would all be over. A deeper, insane urge flashed through him. Momentarily he became afraid he would never see her again. He wanted to extend the agony just a little longer before being released with a chuckle and a pat on the back. He wanted to be her prisoner, just a little longer.

"We can't have you running around badmouthing our employees, can we?" She sounded almost reasonable. Her right hand left his cheek, nestled in the hair at the back of his head, caressing him for an instant. Robert closed his eyes.

Her fingers, entwined in his hair, tightened suddenly and she snapped Robert's head back, and his eyes shot open. She lowered her face over his and Robert thought—oh, briefly—she was going to kiss him. Her mouth would be hot and wet, like a jungle. He anticipated the contact.

"Worm," she said and her inviolate mouth pursed to a sneer.

"Look," Robert said, half-strangled.

"Your time to talk is over," she said, pulling harder on his hair. "Your time to talk is history. It's Babylon. It's Persia."

She had Robert's head in a death grip. He believed his hair was beginning to tear. He raised an arm in a halfhearted attempt at freeing himself only to find her knee quickly in his crotch. She wiggled it in tight and pressed firmly on his most tender center.

She looked intently into his eyes one last time and released him with a dismissive gesture. She stood and straightened her suit.

Again the face showed its feral smile and then she was at the door and there were hands on Robert and he was being dragged down the corridor and, before he could protest, he was thrown into a room and the door was closed.

Robert looked at his cell, with a searching eye, still dazzled from the rough handling, tempering his outrage. He was looking for signs of comfort, for a human touch, for a feeling that here he could sort things out. There was a certain relief to being left alone.

It was a small room, but it was well-appointed. There was a couch (which Robert found out later was a HideA-B-ed), a wash basin, a commode, a chair such as one might find in chain motel rooms, a plastic plant in a bucket. No window. No television. No books.

Other than the aforementioned plant—what was it supposed to resemble, a palm, eucalyptus?—the only nod to aesthetics was a cheap art reproduction Scotch-taped to the back of the door: Breughel's *The Fall of Icarus*.

Robert stretched out on the couch and tried to order his thoughts. He had been insulted, mocked, embarrassed, roughly treated, and, finally, thrown into a small room, apparently to frighten him. He took several deep breaths. Okay, he told himself, overall it wasn't that bad. He had not been physically hurt. What they intended to do with him was a mystery but they would surely come back and talk to him further. Perhaps she would come again. Perhaps they could start over. This was all a misunderstanding. It could be rectified.

When they slid his evening meal under the door was the first time Robert noticed the slit in the door fashioned just for that purpose. And, for the first time, Robert felt nauseatingly afraid. He was actively sick into his commode and the food was left there to spoil. The next morning—had he slept? Had he really slept here all night?—another tray of food was passed under the door and Robert understood he was to slide the old plate out. This he did.

That morning the eggs and sausage looked highly edible and Robert cleaned the plate, again sliding his dishes back out when he was finished. At lunch the process was repeated.

As the days went by Robert realized the real test facing him would be the lack of human contact, and this interested and amused him. He spoke to no one and no one spoke to him. He tried once to shout through the door when his dinner plate arrived but there was no reply.

After many months Robert's routine became sacred. He slept eight hours every night and in the morning made the bed back into a couch. He was disciplined. Once, when the lunch plate was not delivered until midafternoon, Robert grew restless and morose. But he was immediately cheered when the food arrived, especially since his desert was tapioca pudding.

One day was like the next, soldiering on into the unforeseeable future, and Robert found himself living an inner life which surprised him with its richness. His imagination became a flexible, athletic, living thing. He kept his senses alive, his brain sharp. Sometimes he thought of Gayla, but he knew she was young and strong and would make it without him. He smiled a rueful smile and wished her well.

His diet was good thanks to his keepers and he even exercised. His body became an important part of him, no longer just a tool for mobility, but a soul-cage, and he began to marvel daily at the imposing size of his chest and the slate-hard curve of his thighs.

He stayed alive and alert and at the ready. Someday, again, soon perhaps, something would happen to Robert, again a twist, a curve in life's numinous and pedagogic road, and this thing which happened would gladden and astound him. Maybe *she* would return, or maybe it would be something else. But Robert stayed ready, alone in his room beneath the supermarket, a coiled spring of possibility.

Character

Tom Meniscus, at first, did not realize that he had found the secret backstairs to the bedroom of his best friend Rolland Hanson's sister, Katelynn, who was both an invalid and a pink pants, so it was rumored, until he saw the cracked door and its buttery sliver of light and saw the upright, glimmering form of the young woman's perfectly orbicular mammaries, clad only in diaphanous bedgown, nor did he know what he should do with this information except that he must keep it from his roommates, Jeff and Jerry Kinnoson, who were known around campus as party boys with forceful sexual proclivities, including the near-rape of a nubile, freshman bookbuster, according to some sources outside their fraternity ΣAE, not to mention from Katelynn's dipsomaniacal mother, Kathe, and her brutish father, Ron, Congressman Hester's aide, which amounted to a real test of Tom Meniscus's character, I'm telling you.

My Friend, Bob Canaletto

I wanted to write a story about my friend, Bob Canaletto, the plumber. I wanted to describe his rise to grandeur, to the pinnacle of plumberness. How did he do it? Why him and not a dozen other plumbers, equally talented, equally blessed?

I wanted to discuss the "right place at the right time" theory, to debunk it, in a way. There is genius and there is everyone else, and no one, least of all me, admittedly, understands where that demarcation lies. I wanted to say something about that, and about Bob, as a person, as a friend, godfather to my young daughter, Dido. So much has been written about him as a star, as the brightest plumber of his generation.

He has been revered, delineated, deconstructed, and, for all that, misunderstood. His rightfully famous "Burr Removal Treatise" has been reprinted more times than "Desiderata," but few have taken the time to comprehend what he was really saying. Ditto for his "Drain Snake Dialogue: A Lucubration."

But, what about the spiritual Bob Canaletto? What about the philosophical side to this worker in sanitary ware? Was his belief in metempirics consistent with his handling of flux and solder? Did his "God" create his likeness with lampblack, plumber's soil? As of now, this has not been plumbed, if you'll forgive the play on words.

Now that he's gone, has anyone stood up to say, "I knew Bob Canaletto, and he was more than a great pipe cleaner"? I wanted to be that person. I wanted to add my voice to the multitudes crying his name.

I wanted the real Bob to emerge from the sciamachy of myth. Did I know Bob Canaletto better than anyone else knew Bob? This does not interest me. I claim no personal glory.

I wanted to set Bob free.

But this cannot happen now. The zealots and the coven of family members and "friends," the sycophants and arcanists, have had their say. The papers are sealed, the gag order issued, the libraries mute.

But I know. I have my memories, like freshly milled dreams. I sit quietly now and replay them. My sweet memories of my friend, Bob Canaletto.

Delitescent Selves

[A short piece of fiction disguised as a book review]

Delitescent Self: A Sort of Autobiography *by Lark Partee*
W. W. Norton ($26.00)

Reviewed by Resole McRey

The famous American writer, Lark Partee, author of the novels *Don't Put Me in a Nursing Home* and *A Devil of a Time*, among others, has now penned his autobiography, made all the more gladly received by the author's renowned reclusiveness. You know the story: he hasn't been seen in public, no photographs of him exist. So one marvels that such an eremitic spook would even publish a personal history.

First off, as we know, Lark Partee is the author's pseudonym and nowhere in this purposely cryptic and arcane confession does Partee reveal his real name, nor does he talk at all about his early life and family. In passing he does remark, "I was bullied as a child. In the 40's, in America, there was only one thing for a male child to be and that was tough. I was not tough. I was slight, wispy, dreamy, and distracted. I was easy prey." One must intuit the life between the lines, so to speak.

Like Salinger and Pynchon, Partee apparently began to duck the limelight immediately, at the outset of his writing career. In 1958—Partee must have been, what, twenty-two or so?—a slim, first novel appeared from Farrar, Straus and Cudahy, entitled *Blast*. It was the first appearance of the ghostly authorial signature, "By Lark Partee." It seemed to come from nowhere. There was a jape for an author's photo, showing the back of a man's head. And the publisher was either in on the ruse or outside of it like the rest of us. At any rate, the novel was an immediate success, becoming the year's number one bestseller—an aberration for such a literary, experimental first book—and quickly becoming a perennial assignment in college English classes. Its tale of a boy with the head of a donkey, trapped either in a village of cruel idiots, or in his own imagination—there are two schools of thought—struck a chord. The book is probably more discussed than read.

In *Delitescent Self* he dismisses his freshman effort as "that silly book that was embraced by silly people who thought they saw in it a reflection of themselves or the author or both." An odd assessment for a book that established him as one of the up-and-coming authors of the sixties. And the money from the book, Partee admits, aided him in his desire to hide.

But it would be seven years before another book was released and it was the universally panned *Callous*. A long-winded, Joycean, self-indulgent rewriting of ancient mythology, its initial print of 50,000 copies (a monumental count by sixties' standards) was almost immediately remaindered and, for Partee collectors today, it is difficult to find a pristine copy without the telltale scarlet slash on the top edge.

By 1965 readers had embraced a bevy of new writers, Updike, Roth, Mailer, Oates, and Partee was clearly on the outer boundary of this kind of quintessentially American writing. Partee's oeuvre, whatever else one may say about it, stands clearly outside *any* school. When, a few years later he was lumped with the postmodernists, Barth, Barthelme, or Hawkes, he released *A Devil of a Time*, a sentimental story of love gone wrong, of love displaced, and finally of love rediscovered. A six-hundred--page opus, a straightforward soap opera, more Michener than Broch, it was an instant bestseller, outselling the nearest competition by 2 to 1, though the critics were strongly divided on its literary merit.

Here, Partee calls it his "favorite work of the imagination; perhaps the only work I ever did that fully employed my clockwork-like imagination and my clockwork-like heart. I still love the book and others do, also." This last addendum seems strange. What others is he speaking of? His wife, if he has one? His friends, his readers? And does he truly believe this his best work or is this just more obfuscation?

Certainly there is more literature than life in *Delitescent Self*,

Certainly there is more literature than life in *Delitescent Self*, yet Partee even shies away from revealing too much about his creative process. He takes years between books but does not explain why this is so. In mid-disclosure he makes this statement: "Novels are play. I play. I let my mind go a-wandering, like a boy in a dark wood, a fairy tale wood, where one is just as likely to meet a lonely princess as Old Harry. If I could not continue this childish activity I would cease to exist, inasmuch as I seem to exist now."

Masks upon masks. It seems Partee wants us to believe with him, like the dying Tinkerbell. He almost begs us to peek behind the curtain yet he maintains a death-like grip upon the edges of the material. He keeps his cards, and they may be tools of divination, close to the chest.

Yet, for all the shadow play, for all the concealment, for all the adumbration and hide-and-seek, what emerges from this odd unbosoming, this "sort of autobiography," is a man at odds with the world, a man alive—or so he believes—only on the page. It is an absolution, a Catholic sacrament, if one reads the clues sprinkled like breadcrumbs throughout the text. One hypothesizes, connecting the dots, that strict Catholic parents, perhaps in a small town, raised Lark Partee, and perhaps he fled from them with their disapprobation ringing in his ears. The only clear reference that supports this is in "Chapter Two: Real Life," and, though it is scant, it is telling. Partee says, "My folks will never read my books. Papal law shall forbid it." But there are other, more ambiguous intimations concerning this "escape."

Between *A Devil of a Time* and his next book, the strange, metaphysical *Dr. Dee's Assistant*, a gap of ten years. Partee calls these years, "My wandering Jew years. My time in the desert." Whatever happened during this period of silence the result was a book that many critics point to as the work that established Partee as part of the modern canon, and he began to be mentioned with Barth and Mailer and Gaddis and Roth. William Pritchard, in *The New York Times Book Review*, called *Dr. Dee's Assistant* "a work of transcendent beauty, as if light were distilled and reconfigured as alphabetiforms, a book that goes deep into the soul of modern man and is not afraid of what it finds there."

In *Delitescent Self*, Partee calls the book "a poot. Something to do while my mind did other things." Surely, he is hiding again behind a vizard of perversity, flying in the face of his own reputation.

The later books are generally regarded as a downward slope, a diminution of his creative powers. These books were produced quickly, appearing annually: *Rankle, The Art of Diamond Mining*, and his last work, *Don't Put Me in a Nursing Home*. These seem tired exercises or "idea" books, stillborn and with little to recommend them. It was also during this period that he novelized the screenplay to Jacque Dormay's noir thriller, *The Gun Also Rises*. Again, one wonders what the quixotic man of letters was thinking. Though entertaining on the surface, this "hackwork" lacks any real spark.

Another period of silence followed and then this book appeared like Banquo's ghost, an apparition from the past. Partee is still highly regarded for his earlier work but one wonders what this paradoxical attempt at autobiography will do to his reputation. Not that it matters a damn to the man, who must now be approaching seventy*. Near the end of this book he says, "It's a long drink of tepid water, life. For every fizgig there are days of dormant inactivity, of ennui. Women, writing, and gardening have kept me sane, kept whatever neurons firing that still fire. I am grateful for this, YHTD."

And then, as a coda, he adds: "I am through with the game. Let the savage gods take the stage. If I ever held the baton I hereby pass it on. As Jesus said, 'It is over.'" A rather galling bit of egomania.

His publisher is said to be collecting Partee's analects, his letters, his notebooks, for a possible last work, a period to the convoluted sentence Partee has been writing his whole life. When this is released perhaps it will reveal more than this "autobiography," the least revealing book of its kind since Graham Greene's. Lark Partee, whoever you are, wherever you are, you were once a gale in the mild weather of modern writing. Perhaps we shouldn't ask for more from you, more than you are willing to give. Like the Salinger ghouls, your fans seem more intrigued with your invisibility than your books, and this is a sad thing. The camouflage you have chosen to hide behind is a gossamer invention, like Salome's veils. It teases and reveals little. It distracts from your genuine importance, that eccentric body of work—no two books seem to have anything in common, as if written by divers and dissimilar writers (perhaps you are a committee!)—which is unlike any other in American letters.

* Mr. McRey is no mathematician as the years he has quoted in his review do not jibe. [ed.]

Strangers in Love

"It's a beautiful day," Ron said, pocketing a stone.

"You always say that," Allison returned.

"Well," Ron capitulated.

"There are no stores open anywhere. What kind of town is this?"

"I like this town."

"You would."

Allison stood on her toes and peered down the road where a wind soughed like an old dream or a congregation of whispers.

"Maybe we should move on," she said.

"Let's not be hasty," Ron said.

They walked. Ron started to take Allison's hand. It was an old impulse. It had been a long time since he had done so. Her hand used to fit his like a pistol. They used to always hold hands. Holding hands now was as out of the question as Mormonism or group sex. Ron thought about something else.

"Dead," Allison said.

"Mm," Ron mmed.

"I'll only walk a bit longer," Allison huffed.

"Just up around this corner here," Ron said, although the corner did not look promising. It looked like an ex-corner, a place of ripe dissatisfaction.

At the corner the couple looked in four directions but neither of them the same one at the same time. Desolation has its own sound, its own way of being. It stood in front of them like the Colossus.

"Well," Ron said.

"Shit," Allison proposed.

"There's another town a few miles down the highway. I think I saw a sign."

Allison stood still, her emotions wrinkled and desiccated, her face a modernized Virgin Mary.

"Shit," she finally said, unaware, probably, that she was repeating herself.

"Allison," Ron said, her name feeling odd in his mouth like a new retainer. It had been years since he'd said it quite this way.

Allison could perhaps not have heard him. Perhaps she didn't.

"I'm in love with someone else," Allison said at last.

Ron looked down the off-white side street. He thought he saw a sign lit up, a paint store full of colors.

"This is not turning out the way I planned," Ron said.

"Well," Allison answered him.

"There are plenty more towns," Ron said. "I've been in plenty of towns. Most have motels, nice little motels in pastels and with a pool lit at night. I've slept in many different beds."

There was a bad stillness. The air was black or appeared so.

"I guess I'll just live in a new town," Ron said.

"What about me? What about me? What about me?" Allison keened.

But Ron had already moved on, setting up his things in a new apartment, putting his CDs in alphabetical order, studying each of his books as he shelved them. It was a nice apartment if you didn't look behind things. Ron thought his life here could be different. He thought it needed to be, maybe.

A Small Fire

The man built a small fire ostensibly to keep warm. There was no breeze next to the deserted highway, but the air was filled with prickly wintriness. He found dry brush, discarded wrappers, civilization's detritus. It burned humbly, a hermit's chauffer.

He squinted toward the horizon. The view was bleak, a long stretch of emptiness, relieved by withered trees and scrub grass. Above there was a gibbous moon and a scattering of stars.

He opened the wallet, pulled out the sheaf of bills, folded them, and secreted them in his shirt. In amongst the bills were small bits of paper he had to pick out, oddments upon which were jotted notes. "Swan Lake Barbie for Kitten." And, "Find duffel bag." Arcane messages from someone else's life, alive in their strangeness.

And another, older scrap, almost worn away by its time within the bill pouch. It felt soft, tatty, decomposing paper turned to fur. Upon it a single, blurry word: "Rachel." In one small wad he consigned these esoteric, ultimately meaningless comments to his fire.

The credit cards were lined up like bright toys, multicolored and still crisp; he fingered each in its slot before removing them one by one. He was torn between reverence and aversion. These simple cards carried too much connotation, too much information: hope, loss, renewal, and waste. He relished how their edges blackened, curled, bent inward as he laid them carefully on the fire. The flames now guttered so he sought more dry brush to keep them going.

Once the fire renewed itself the man sat back down on an overturned crate. He rededicated himself to the contents of the wallet. The fire now sizzled and smelled of melted plastic.

Insurance card, country club membership card, social security, a lawyer's business card, a sandwich shop's tally, voter's registration. One life, so many tendrils, so many lifelines.

After burning these the man discovered a clever hidden part of the wallet. The blackened nail of his forefinger sought its concealed secrets. He removed a neatly folded piece of paper, within which were more folded notes and a single photograph. The newness of this find spoke of a more recent squirreling away. The outer piece of paper, apparently a fine writing stock, was blank. The folded papers within were letters, three to be exact. The script was feminine. The words made the man squirm: passionate, seductive, furtive, private. They were all signed, "R." The man flung them onto the flame and simultaneously brought the photograph closer to his face, maneuvering it so that his hand did not block the light from his solitary crematory.

The woman's face was lovely, dove-like. He could almost feel the down of her cheek, the moist corner of her lipsticked lips. So, it was with slight regret that he laid it also upon the pyre and watched the fire eat it, first with a quick black center burst and then, rapidly, from the edges in.

There were other pictures, a wife, and two children. The wife was pretty, self-consciously so. There were a number of pictures of each child, nesting dolls of varying age. Flip them quickly and they were a nickelodeon, telling a story about how soon they are grown and gone. For one flashing moment the family blazed to life in his head, whole. Then this passed. The man let the photographs slip through his fingers and tumble soundlessly into the fire.

The driver's license stubbornly stuck in its slit pocket. The man irritably pulled it loose. He brought it close to his whiskered chin. Numbers, letters, and symbols: data. As if this code bespoke a life. The weight was off by a good decade. Eyes: blue? Class: D? What did that mean? Dates: the renewal time was soon—only a few weeks away. The picture on the license was a good one, showing a strong jaw, a fierce eye. It said, Here is a man used to control. Here is a good man, a hardworking man. A family man, yet with uncertainties. Each of us has his or her own secrets, our own places of clouded mystery. He liked the man's face, as he had before. The license ignited with a small *pop* as its plastic unsealed. The paper beneath was quickly consumed.

The wallet itself, a leather, burned haltingly, poorly, as if it were flesh itself, and the stench of it was nauseating. The man rose into the frosted air, stretching himself like a cat. The night would soon give way to morning. He had a long way to go.

Harry Styrene and the Holy Virgin

Harry Styrene had worked at the bookstore since a teenager. Now, at twenty-seven, he loved books the way most men loved a woman or God. Harry had come to the business a naïf and, after listening to the smarter customers the store catered to, he had learned the names and works of the modern masters: Updike, Roth, Bellow, Garcia Marquez, Murdoch, Fowles.

These books opened doors in Harry. Where once was a man like a plastered wall, solid but blank and uninspiring, there now was a learnéd and worldly fellow who could quote from contemporary literature as if from the gospels. Often he held a stranger's gaze and, with a lightning-rod finger raised, he would reel off a quote verbatim, ending with a name as solid as a period.

"Anthony Burgess," he might say and look intently at his audience until they nodded or walked away. Harry felt good at these times. He felt as if he were making a difference.

So, though he was still often lonely, and his flesh ached like a sore tooth, he was content. Knowing a new Rabbit novel or another lovely Muriel Spark awaited him when he got off work assuaged some of the desperation of his position. Ah, books! Ah, humanity!

So it may seem that The Powers that Be made an eccentric decision sending the Virgin Mary to Harry's apartment one sere autumn evening as Harry prepared a potpie and a soda for his bachelor's dinner. Harry was just snapping the legs of a TV tray into place when light surrounded him from behind; he was spotlit.

He spun and there she was, just as if she had transported from the Starship Enterprise. Yet, she was as solid as the eternal rocks.

She was beautiful in her white raiment and corn silk hair. Her skin was the color of the dogwood blossom and her eyes were periwinkles. She smiled at Harry as if they were old friends. Harry clutched his chest in melodramatic pantomime, when in truth he was indeed awestruck. But, unpracticed in gesture or pronouncement, Harry could only ape a movie star playing a part.

"Harry," the beautiful vision spoke.

"Grg," Harry said.

"Do you know who I am?"

Harry had no idea. This is what comes of secular reading. Harry had never had religion; it was as foreign to him as the foliage of youth.

"Mother," Harry said, weakly. Harry's mother was not dead, nor was she young and beautiful. She lived in Cincinnati and wrote romance novels at the rate of one per month for a publishing company that paid her by the book. "Mother" was a foolish hypothesis.

Yet the radiant woman said, "Yes. Mother. Mary."

Now Harry wasn't ignorant. It dawned on him pretty quickly what the vision was implying.

"Pshaw," Harry said.

"No. Not pshaw, Harry. I am. I am the Virgin Mary come to you in a vision, a vision as real as early evening lightning, as genuine as butter spread on stale bread."

"Well, why?" Harry rightly asked.

"Because, Harry," the beautiful woman answered and looked for a place to rest her holy hip, settling on the arm of a truly monstrous easy chair. "Because you are godless and we need a messenger."

"Godless."

Harry did not take kindly to the word, regardless of its exactitude.

"Godless," the Virgin Mary repeated. "We use the godless for messages."

"We," Harry said. "Who's we?"

"Harry," Mary said, pursing her perfect lips, the color of seashell.

"You and God?" Harry asked. Finally, he set aside the half-assembled tray.

"Well, for our purposes, let's say, yes. Anyway, you have been chosen to deliver the message."

"Deliver how, sister? It's not like I have my own talk show."

"Oh. Here and there. Hither and thither. Yon. Tell the customers in your store. Tell the checkout girl at the grocery. Word spreads. It's how it's always worked. Well, since the, you know, burning bush thing."

Harry sat down in his La-Z-Boy. He ran a hand over his face as if he were washing away dreams. When he looked up she was still there, beautiful and shining and as resplendent as love. Or evil.

"Okay," Harry said. "Sure. I'll do it."

"That's the spirit," the Virgin M. said. "Come here, Harry."

Harry rose slowly from his chair and shuffled toward his uninvited guest. He looked at his feet where black socks hung as loosely as Cossack pantaloons. The Virgin Mary seemed to glow like phosphorous, white though, like a star. Harry was afraid to look directly at her. She took Harry's hand.

Electricity flowed into him. A feeling like pure joy flooded his whole body as if it had been injected with a hypodermic. Her face was so lovely it hurt.

"I knew you were right," she said to him, smiling, well, beatifically.

"Wh-what's the message?" Harry said. His eyes were locked on hers. He couldn't have looked away if his life depended on it, as it may very well have. Her smile was a promise, a deep promise.

"Here it is," she said. "Ignore the media. Life is still full of miracles."

Harry blinked a few times.

"That's it," he said. He couldn't help sounding disappointed.

"That's your message, yes. We do this all the time, sweetheart. Little messages, small steps. From a small acorn a mighty oak grows."

"Right," Harry said.

It was then the Virgin Mary stood and Harry stumbled a bit backward. Her hand still held his. The warmth still flowed into him and he was still comforted, peaceful, happy.

Mary leaned over—and though this was not in the usual realm of her duties—she kissed Harry.

That is how Harry got the birthmark on his cheek in the shape of a mouth. And that is how he became a spokesperson for YHTD, simply by being home when His Hallowed Harbinger called. Just that modestly, Harry Styrene became one of the chosen, a Holy Fool.

Mystical Participation

"The primordial image, or archetype, is a figure—be it a daemon, a human being, or a process—that constantly recurs in the course of history and appears wherever creative fantasy is freely expressed."

—*Carl Jung*

"My dear Jung, promise me never to abandon the sexual theory…we must make a dogma of it, an unshakable bulwark."

—*Sigmund Freud*

Gus called me up, a rare-enough occurrence.
"I need you to come with me. I'm collecting," he began.
"Uh huh," I said. It was before coffee.
"Can   you?"
"Sure. What are we collecting?"
"Unconsciousness."

"Right." I knew to give Gus enough rope. He went off on toots occasionally and it was best just to humor him.

"Of the entire race. Why I need your help."

"I guess you do," I said.

"Can you?"

"Sure, sure. When do you wanna start?"

"Right away, this morning if you can."

"Lemme get a few things done around here. About eleven?"

Gus allowed as how eleven would be okay. I didn't really have a lot to do, but I knew it was best to give Gus some time to reflect. On more than one occasion his initial enthusiasm for an idea waned after he'd had his morning bowel movement.

"It's collective, not collected," my wife said.

"What?" I blinked.

"The joke doesn't work."

"Oh." She had stung me. While never my most enthusiastic cheerleader, she normally gave me a polite pass.

"The joke is your whole premise, hence the story doesn't work."

To be honest she had never been supportive of my little literary career (her diminutive), even after the novel. Sure, publicly she had expressed glee. Ostensibly this was the best thing that had ever happened to me, us. She was the doting wife. The helpmate. Privately it was a different story. She wasn't hostile to my intentions—except when my "writing day" interfered with something she thought I should be doing. She was, and this hurts more, indifferent.

My name is James Royce. You probably remember my one afternoon in the sun, my academic novel, *Schooled Royal.* It made a small splash, the kind of splash that only happens in the shallow end. Kirkus called it "a good flirt." My friend, the Jewish novelist, Shlomo Einstein, said, "With a pitch-perfect sonata of voices recalling the experiments of Nicholson Baker and William Gaddis, *Schooled* is a bittersweet gospel for our time." My most oft-quoted blurb. Who can resist a good blurb?

But, it's been three years since *Schooled* was released and all I have accomplished is one short story in *Cranky* called "Notes Toward the Story," a do-it-yourself grab bag of story ideas that said more about its author's disarray than it did about experimental deconstruction. And I had a poem in *American Poetry Review*, a poem called "Strictly Blowjob," whose history is best not measured.

So, here I sit. Trying to make a story out of a joke, a joke my wife has informed me works about as well as an unreplenished stream. My eyes hurt—something behind them wasn't right. And my fingers felt stiff, perhaps because it was cold in our house, drafty. I tried—

By the time I reached Gus's A-frame he was outside in the driveway, leaning against his Pontiac.

"I guess you're ready to go," I said, grinning foolishly.

"C'mon," he said. Gus was intense—it was his defining principle. This intensity made him one of the best analysts in Zurich. Dr. Jung of Zurich—the Castor to Dr. Freud's Pollux. Or, better perhaps, the yin to his yang.

We took Gus's battered Pontiac into the city. He was an indifferent driver, indifferent to the ebb and flow of traffic, seemingly indifferent to the possibility of an injurious crash. He talked as he drove.

He concluded: "And that's where we need to begin, I believe, at the university, among the lithe limbs and torsos of the youthful. Where better to measure the consciousness of the race?"

"I'm with you, Gus," I said, around a half-masticated donut. "What's the process? I mean, you got like instruments, geigometers or whatnot?"

"Hm," he said, and his hesitation made me blanch. Another wild-goose chase, I assumed.

Finally, he said, "We're fishing for archetypes. Okay? Now, archetypes, they have to be rooted out, like truffles. The unconscious needs to be plumbed as if it were a piece of ground full of elusive buried riches. What we use, in each case, will be determined by the individual. Okay?"

I could only say, "Okay—"

"It would help," my wife said, "if you had some understanding of Jungian psychology. Wouldn't it? And, also, of Zurich. You can't set your story in Zurich in the early 1900s if you have no feel for the place. What's with the modern car, lingo, etc.?"

Clearly, I was going to have to stop showing my pages to my wife.

Now, for you out there unmarried, or perhaps married but oblivious to its various undulations and sea changes, I formulate this encomium: my wife is a wonderful wife. She is. Effie is a good woman, who, through years of living with a writer who is both abstracted and severe—if I may characterize myself in this way—has been driven into a certain blind alley of her customary personality, a blind alley which includes the desire to decimate my confidence as a creative person. Apparently.

"Well," I attempted, "the story is a, what, experimental, possibly humorous, mock-CV? If you can see it that way—"

"Jim, sweet—" She cut me off. "Even so, one needs a *grounding* in subject matter. Take the time to do the research— if you want to parody something you need to know it inside and out. Know its strengths, weaknesses, places of vulnerability—"

"If you've been following my writing at all over the past ten years, you would know I'm working in what I might call anti-research burlesque."

"Uh huh," she said, in that way of hers. An "uh huh" that transported more than its five letters and a space should be able to transport. Then she smiled a tight, light smile. She turned her back to me and stepped into our closet to get dressed.

I could only stare after her. Her now-denuded back, with its moles and strawberry marks, was a lovely thing to behold. The way it sloped down to begin her fine rear end never failed—even after all these years—to stir me.

"Effie," I said, weakly. I was disappearing.

Gus swung the car onto campus. It was a bright, spring day, and all around us walked the beautiful children of modern Zurich. They were clearly the master race and I felt foolish for interrupting their glittering existence.

Gus was armed with only a notebook, a pen, and his charming smile.

"This way," he said, as if it mattered.

He stopped the first lovely co-ed he came across, a young woman of indeterminate age—she could be sixteen or twenty—a young woman with hair made of pure light.

"Excuse me," he said.

She fixed us with a practiced hauteur.

"I'm conducting a scientific survey. Could I trouble you for a bit of your time?"

"Survey?" she said.

"Right. I just need to ask you a few questions and record what you say and we go from there."

"Sure," she said, a sparkling jewel to make Europe proud.

Her name was Joy Jacobi and she was majoring in biology. Dr. Jung and I accompanied her to a room in the copious student center on campus, a semi-private room with tables and chairs. Dr. Jung seemed to know about these rooms beforehand—perhaps he had been conducting these experiments for years.

Dr. Jung put the sweet co-ed through a labyrinth of questions, mostly about her dreams, which she remembered too clearly. I suspected she was entertaining us, spinning out exciting scenarios to spice up the interview. Joy had a quick and creative mind.

"And I'm at an outdoor amphitheater, on stage. The audience is all men, sports stars, and actors. And I'm naked—" Here Joy touched the button of her shirt between her breasts. "And I'm enjoying being ogled—the men are clearly excited by my body. So I'm holding my breasts, offering them up, my nipples hard between my fingers. And the men, as one, take their stiff members out—and I'm looking at a crowd of beautiful erect phalluses—and my excitement grows until I'm touching my honey box. Then one man mounts the stage—his large member in his hand—"

"Always with the sex," Effie says.

I had vowed not to show her anything else I'd written. But she had gone to the computer and pulled the file up uninvited.

"You turn every story toward sex."

"It's one of my themes, yes."

"It's not a theme, Jim. It's a prurient obsession. An author has a responsibility toward his characters, like a parent toward the child. It's literary rape is what it is."

"That's a little strong, isn't it? I write about sex because it's a major topic. It is the mystery inside us all. We have to investigate it. D. H. Lawrence said—"

"You aren't investigating, you're seducing your own creations. It's date rape!" Here she laughed. At least that.

"Thanks, dear," I said, with a bitter moue. I put the book I was reading—Goncharov's *The Same Old Story*—closer to my face, signaling that I was through talking. She had cut me again. I sulked in my Russian apologue.

I, James Royce, remembered a night from early in my marriage. Effie had taken longer than usual coming to bed. When she emerged from the bathroom she had on the most outrageously sexy outfit she had ever commandeered. Very brief panties—strings and a patch, really—a bustier I think they call it—and cowboy boots! A laugh escaped before other ambitions took over.

"Ef-ffie," I had sputtered.

"You've sprung a leak, husband mine," she said.

"I've sprung more than that," I riposted, and pulled back the sheet to show her a knoll of appreciation.

"Mm, hm," she said. "I like. All that just for this—" and here she wiped a palm over her whole provocative tenement.

Then she had moved sinuously toward me—the memory is bittersweet in its singularity. I pulled my pajama bottoms aside and was revealed. She moved her whole erotic length against me, and, in the process, palmed my erection, a deft-enough move.

As she began to pump it slowly, with a seemingly new genius, she whispered in my ear, "Don't write about *this*, asshole."

Gradually, our "interviews" took on the nature of a fever dream. It became clear to me that Dr. Jung had other things in mind than amassing the *collective* unconscious. Or he had become dangerously sidetracked.

"Ah, the slim, untouched bodies of youth, eh?" he allowed on the third morning of our collecting adventure. "A science beyond science, heh heh."

We began luring young co-eds to his dusty apartment. And once there it wasn't long before Dr. Jung had insinuated them out of their fashionable garments. Some of these young people seemed anxious to further science inquiry in whatever way necessary—such was Gus's reputation. Others—and I will relate the tale of one such minx—wanted the titillation of it. Thrill seekers, Dr. Jung labeled them.

It was with one such thrill seeker, on one sultry afternoon in sultry Zurich, that it came to a head, so to speak. Her name was Patty Bourgeois. She dressed like a hooker—or the approximation of a hooker for on-campus purposes. And she arrived at Gus's *appartement* smoking a cigarette, striding in with the confidence of unbroken youth.

"I hear we're studying things formerly hidden here, my good doctor," Patty said through a veil of smoke. Her cockiness did not bother Gus. He smiled like an adder.

"Yes, my dear," he simpered. "We're gonna enter the dream world. Your dream world."

It was his standard patter, but with Patty it seemed iniquitous. I wanted no part of this—yet I could not leave. Was it loyalty, friendship? Was it pure animal desire? I lobbied for my better half to take over. My better half was on holiday. I was priapic, I admit. Animal, anima. What was at work, I halfheartedly grilled myself.

Patty Bourgeois was short work. She was eager to get to the good part.

"And in this dream, Patty, you desire these men?"

"Oh, yes, Doctor."

"Both of them—in this, what, strange, darkened cave?"

"Both, Doctor. And how."

Patty Bourgeois was playing a dangerous game. Yet, I wanted to go with her. God help me I did.

"Now Patty, we will act out this dream. Okay? We will strip down to your basic shadow self, yes? We will move from thinking, feeling, intuition, to sensation. Are you with me?"

"Yes, Doctor, anything." Her trance-state was unconvincing.

"Show me, Patty, just what your dream is like. I want you to—"

Patty was already pulling her shirt over her head. I swallowed, an insensate assistant. She was naked before my saliva hit the floor. She had breasts like sea swells, thighs crimson with heat.

"You are naked?"

"You're so *intuitive*, Doctor. I *love* that."

Dr. Jung smiled his demon smile.

"Tell us what these dream lovers do for you, Patty. Show us your dream."

Patty Bourgeois did not hesitate. Patty Bourgeois unbuckled Dr. Jung's pants and pulled his sizeable manhood out into the fusty air. Jung is hung, I couldn't help thinking.

"Aaah," Dr. Jung said. It was the most unmedical *aah* of his career.

As she began to fondle him in earnest and Gus began taking off his shirt, Patty's sensuous eyes met mine.

"Come here, Igor," she said. "Get behind me."

"Oh, for Christ's sake," Effie howled. "This is beyond the pale, even for you. You're sinking—willingly—into pornography. And your prose shows it. This is third-rate Cinemax coupling."

Goddamit. I had hidden the manuscript. Created a fictitious file called *Lyrical and Critical Essays*. She was uncanny in her ability to discover it.

"You're just jerking off," she continued. "I mean, this isn't for other eyes, right? You presumably are working on this between more serious projects."

I smiled my weak-cat smile. The one I use when I want to hit someone.

"It's an experiment," I began.

"Right," she cut me off, her hand actually making a downward axe stroke. "The investigation to discover how horny you are." She laughed at least.

I could have countered that if I were horny the responsibility might be partly hers. I did not.

"Where is this going?" she softened.

I took the bait. She was playing good cop/bad cop, playing both parts herself. She smiled encouragement.

"Um, I'm trying to steer it in the direction of—" I was cornered. I had no idea what to say. In truth the story had no plan. My stories never did. I began with a line and if it took me someplace the fishing was good. If it didn't I still got to sit in the sun by the river.

Perhaps this is what I should have told her.

"Let's make it simpler," Effie said. "I think I can help you with this. What happens next—I mean, right here—what happens next? After 'Get behind me.'"

"Um," I fumbled. "He gets behind her."

"Riding the train," Effie laughed, in playful mode.

"Yes," I laughed, too. I was trying to relax.

"So, they've got the threesome going, Dr. Jung, this surely buxom and nubile co-ed, and his assistant, who is a stand-in for you, right?"

"Yes," I said, warming, both to literary alchemy and fleshly pursuits.

"What does she say?" Effie asked, placing the pages on my desk and seating herself on a hassock.

"What does she say?" I repeated Effie's query to stall for time. Could I write for a woman under a woman's scrutiny? Effie thought I was letting her fill in the blank.

"Oh, Igor, yes, like that. Hold me by the ass."

Gulp, I said. To myself.

"Okay," I said, "but she's got Jung's priapus in her mouth."

"Cock," Effie said.

"Cock," I parroted. "How can she talk?"

"She's talking around it, so to speak."

"Okay."

"Take it out and show it to me."

I was hard, readers, hard as a piece of the nether millstone. Just like that. It was not unusual for me to arouse myself writing—sometimes I think, partly, this is why I write. To animate myself. I reached for my zipper.

Effie laughed. "I was miming the co-ed," she snorted. She actually snorted. "Sorry, dear, I was saying she could say to her rearward partner, 'take it out and show it to me.'"

"Of course," I said, rezipping.

"But then again," Effie said. "Take it out and show me, Jim."

I looked long and thoughtfully at my wife. I wanted to understand what was going on. I wanted her to see me as the contemplative man I was. I also wanted to fuck her.

She put her hand over my crotch, giving with the limpid eyes. She kneaded me for a minute.

"This is exciting for you, isn't it?"

"Mm hm."

"I mean, this whole creation thing, this whole godlike creation thing, where you control your characters like puppets, pornographic puppets. It's so Jungian, I see now. The literal dream and the symbolic dream, the sensation function, the anima, animus, the yin, yang. I see what you're doing, where you're going with this experiment. I think I can help you, would you like that? You know, there's more to you maybe than I imagined. Isn't that a funny thought after all the time we've been together? I think I haven't spent enough time admiring your mind, your mind's eye, your powers of castle-building. It's like a fever dream, isn't it? It is interesting, the nexus of literature and sex, titillation. I see why it gets you excited. This is like an epiphany! Making people up is sexy, it really is."

To my wife's credit, during this out-loud introspection, this aside, she never stopped stroking me. It was exegesis as foreplay. She did know where and how to touch me. And, my friends, she pulled me out, right there at my desk, with the blank page nearby, with my imagination fired, she pulled me out and very slowly, like the king's best concubine, lowered her wet mouth onto me. She had not sucked me in a decade. I was a teenager again. And she my new girlfriend, the one I'd always desired.

"Christ," Patty said. "Goddammit."

"Umph," Jung said as his penis fell out of her mouth like a punctured balloon.

The three just stared at each other. Understanding this cosmic coitus interruptus was beyond them, beyond even the magisterial powers of Gustave Jung. It left them moony. It left them fish out of water. Suddenly the air had gone out of the story. With no conscious effort on their part everything just stopped, went south, stillborn like seed sown on rocky ground.

What happened? A failure of the imagination, a failure of nerve? The three were embarrassed, standing there in the all-in-all. Their faces were blank, so blank there is a yen to fill them in.

They are in hell, or perhaps in hell's porte-cochère, a limbo.

They are abandoned gods, spirits left to wander. Though they could not wander.

They could not even move.

Haunted

"Even when I watch TV
There's a hole where you used to be."

—John Lennon

Start the story with its protagonist's name: Bob Plumb. Start with the crux of his problem, the grit asking its oyster to pearl: Bob Plumb is haunted.

He thinks he is haunted.

Say this: he lives by himself. Because his wife left him.

Her name was Honey, really Honey. Given name. Honey Plumb was, by all accounts, a beautiful woman, a leading light in life's drama. She was accustomed to being center stage, when she was younger, for most of her days, when she was Honey Moser.

Why she married Bob is a mystery, one of life's mysteries. He came along at a time when she was floundering a bit. She had been dumped by a man who had just passed his bar exam. Honey had thought, she had been led to think, that her life was achieving shape through the fast-track success plan that graduating from law school represents. Honey Moser thought she was about to marry a successful, wealthy man. This man, this new lawyer, married someone else. Just like that. Honey cursed herself for planning, for attempting to plan, the future. She knew better.

And suddenly, there in her path was this innocuous, fairly attractive man named Bob Plumb, a teacher of English at a private girls' school. Bob Plumb had nice shoulders, a way of walking that was both hesitant and confident. A bounce.

Bob Plumb was also coming out of a relationship with a fellow teacher, a young woman named Linn Bass. Linn, with an "i." Bob was looking moony, standing in Honey Moser's path, looking like a man who had just been kicked in the stomach.

It was in the grocery store, this path, the one that contained both Honey Moser and Bob Plumb. Bob was caressing casabas. He had no idea why he was feeling them, rapping on their firm fruitiness like a spirit knocks on a table. But Bob was not thinking about casabas, their fruitiness, their secrets beneath the skin. Bob was thinking about Linn and her impossibly soft crotch and how once he was welcome there and now would be welcome there no more. And Bob was thinking that this would haunt him for the rest of his days and, looking ahead because we can, we say, yes it will. Let's not foreshadow; let's return to the concrete moment in the produce aisle of Schnuck's grocery store.

"What are you doing?" Honey Moser asked, smiling her sucky-calf smile.

Bob looked up as if the Lord had tapped him on the shoulder.

Honey Moser stood there in the light, a glimmering eidolon.

"I have no idea," Bob answered honestly.

"Put it down and walk away," Honey said, tinkling.

Bob thought perhaps it was time to smile, to chance a smile.

He moved his mouth in a shuttering rictus.

Honey Moser squinted, shifting her lovely weight.

"Sorry, yes," Bob said, putting the casaba down and stepping away from both it and Honey Moser.

"Okay," Honey said, beginning to roll away from this awkward man, this mooncalf.

"You're lovely," Bob said. He just said it.

Honey Moser turned now, her full-on radiance blinding. A simple key, a lucky stab: she had never been called lovely before. Many synonyms but not that particular modifier. It pricked her like a fairy tale spindle.

"Funny man, odd-duck," Honey said.

But she was smiling.

"Yes, sorry," Bob said again. "I'm, I'm beggared, jetsam. This is what's left of a man once loved."

"She broke your heart."

"Yes, she did."

"Join the club," Honey said.

"No," Bob said without thinking. "Not you—"

"Oh, yes. Left behind like a sinner at the rapture."

That night Bob and Honey had their first date. They went to a Cuban restaurant near Bob's home. Afterward she did what babes in the woods do. They assuaged their simple, human loneliness with contact, sweet, fleshly contact.

A month later they were man and wife.

Rick Pozgar was Bob Plumb's best friend. A writer who worked in a bookstore, Rick was the kind of sounding board, empath, that makes for long-term friendships. Bob loved Rick and Rick loved Bob. Sometimes they even said it.

Rick could not believe that Bob had married before Rick had even met the woman. When they finally got together, Rick and his girlfriend, Sandra, and Bob and Honey, the conversation was warm and lively. Rick liked Honey immediately and Sandra and Honey went off during the evening, into the kitchen to build a bond that males could never understand. Honey and Sandra had coffee the next day. They talked lovingly about their men, their funny habits, their goony love affair with each other, even about them sexually.

It was all chirpy and blithe.

It lasted a few months, a few months of sex and shopping and renting videos. And, let's be fair: the sex was good. Bob, for all his distractedness, for all his inertness, for all his exhausted outsiderness, Bob was pretty good in the sack. Not great, but adequate, unselfish. It wasn't that, assassin of so many consanguinities, bad sex. No, one day Honey took a hard look at Bob Plumb and thought, oh, Holy Ghost, I could have made a better match. I'd even prefer one of the dull bankers from the club, thought Honey Plumb.

So, she began disappearing. Afternoons at first and then, as her boldness grew, evenings. Once she even stayed out all night, the night she hooked up with a real estate mogul named Henry De Hart. You can write the scene the next morning at the Plumbs.

"I can't say I didn't see this coming," Rick told Bob a few days later over Mexican food and Tecates.

"Right. Why was she with me? One of the glittering stars."

"That's not what I meant." It was.

"I know." He didn't.

"So, the only question now is, what do you do next?" Rick said, masticating a tough piece of tortilla. Was it tortilla?

"That's not, of course, the only question. I can think of a good-dozen questions, some true-false, some multiple-choice. Some no-choice, no-win, no-contest. So many questions, so little mind."

Rick stared at his plate which was as colorful as a Jackson Pollock dropcloth. He had no advice to offer. Let's be truthful here: when one's friend has had his (or her) heart eviscerated there is only one thing to say. That one thing is: I'm here for you. Beyond that, as friends, we are as useful as monkey fat.

"I'm here for you," Rick said.

Bob grinned a poorly constructed and insincere grin.

So we send Bob home, where he has to take himself in. Home is where the hard is. The house now, for Bob, represented failure, an over-the-precipice-sized failure. The TV only showed movies that Honey loved. The refrigerator still held arcane comestibles that Honey loved: wheat germ, sparrow grass, propolis. The bed was the bed where Honey loved. It was all so defeating, so beyond him. Bob sat in his living room, sunk deep in a chair the color of the bottom of the sea. He sunk badly. In his living room there was no living.

There was no life left for Bob, Bob thought.

Nor had there been much sleep, Morpheus leaving Bob on the same train Honey commandeered.

Somehow, on the fourth night PH (Post Honey), Bob fell into a restless sleep. He dreamt that night that he was lying on the viscous floor of a damp cave. All around him, seemingly sprouting from the floor, writhed tall, blue, transpicuous penises, swaying as if in a gentle breeze. Bob reached out for the one nearest him, a particularly substantial and gnarly example. As he held it in his hand warmth entered his body, an electric reawakening. And indeed it was then that Bob awoke. His head was still in dreamspace. The room seemed overheated, like a greenhouse. He couldn't shake the unsettling vision of his dream, nor the semisweet feeling of that botanic phallus. Suddenly, Bob was physically ill. He barely made it into the bathroom to spill.

Afterward, Bob sat on the cool bathroom floor, a wet washcloth across the back of his neck. It was a brand of comfort Honey had taught him. Naturally, it had felt much better under her gentle ministrations.

Slowly, Bob rose and looked at himself in the mirror over the sink. He looked old and depleted. He used the damp washcloth to wipe his face. Outside, rosy-fingered dawn was turning to the title page, the day's book unwritten. Bob reached for his toothbrush to clean the taste of vomitus from his mouth. Next to his baby-blue brush lay the toothpaste, its little majorette cap nearby. Bob stared at the composition on the edge of the sink for a long minute.

Here's what was odd: Bob always recapped the toothpaste. Bob was fastidious. Bob was anal. To find the cap next to the tube was tantamount to discovering Charybdis in his bathtub. Bob tried to hearken back to the night before. Had he, in his dizzy grief, been so sloppy? Of course that was the answer. Even a man as driven by routine as Bob was has, on occasion, slipped off his well-worn track, if only for a moment. A slip. That's all this represented.

Bob brushed his teeth, recapping the paste tightly.

The daylight was impending regardless of Bob's lack of enthusiasm for it. When Bob shuffled into the kitchen and hit the light switch the bulb blew, a soft purple *pop*. Good morning!

That day passed like a stone. Like jellied brainchild. Bob went to work, bumped into his fellow teachers as if he were a blind man, told his students that love was a poor kinescope, told them that they could read *Harry Potter* instead of *Dubliners* if they were so inclined. He went home that day with absolutely no memory of how the day had gone, what he had done, etc. A dangerous way to run a life, but there it is.

Bob threw some ground beef, some tomatoes, some rice, and some hot sauce into a frying pan and called it dinner. He sat in front of the TV, which was showing a reality series featuring staged cuckoldry. Bob wept soft, warm tears into his dinner. As one show morphed into another Bob just sat and wept. Later, some time later, through his foggy vision he saw a woman on a desert island opening her top for the entire world to see. Her breasts were supple, blurry blobs of sexual tension. Bob felt as if he might explode, as if inside an extraterrestrial was hatching à la *Alien*.

Bob threw the rest of his dinner down the garbage disposal, the same one that quit on him one time because of an overabundance of pasta. He heard the satisfying grinding *swoosh* of a successful disposal and he felt no satisfaction. He leaned on the counter for support: Bob felt as if the edge of forever was at his feet and all he wanted to do was jump.

Then his attention was drawn to the spice rack. Bob loved his spice rack and doted on it, constantly re-alphabetizing it after Honey used it. Here's what arrested Bob's attention: sage was before rosemary. How could that be? Had Honey slipped in unannounced and cooked herself a meal? No, that was foolish. No one had been in Bob's house except Bob for five days now.

Bob gently put the spices back in their customary place. As he did so he felt a slight shudder in his arm as if he had hit his ulnar nerve. Someone or something had rearranged his spice rack. Now, *there* was a foolish thought. But, that's what Bob was thinking as his tears dried up, as his house settled around him like a docked ship, ticking and rocking and trying to right itself. With the world a tilt-a-whirl Bob stumbled to his couch, diving onto it.

Somewhere basketball was being played, Bob thought. On TV. Basketball with its set rules and constant measurements. The basket was 10 feet from the floor. It had always been and it always would be. Bob surfed for a game and in no time landed in Cleveland where LeBron James was king and where, just now, as Bob reeled, LeBron was dunking on some hapless, nameless, muscle-bound power forward from New Jersey. The ship gradually stopped rocking. Bob watched the game for a full hour without ever taking it in. His mind skipped over the surface of the game like a rock on a frozen lake. Something ineffable was eating at him, as if a small rodent was nibbling the edges of his thought. Bob cursed his own clammy metaphors. But, finally, Bob's mind came to rest. He was thoughtless.

Bob slept that night like a baby. No, not crying and peeing himself, but without disturbing dreams or flesh-hungry longings for Honey's return. He woke the next day refreshed. Showered, shat, ate, dressed, drove to school. Only to be confronted by a near-empty campus. Apparently, it was a holiday.

At loose ends, Bob drove round the city, the city where he lived. It was all painful. Every building, every stoplight, every couple locked onto each other like grim death, reminded Bob just how alone he was. Bob was abandoned on a desert island, an island called Home. He had a brief, fleeting impulse to drive his Honda off a cliff. As far as he knew, there were no cliffs nearby.

Bob drove by Rick's. There was a strange car in Rick's driveway, a Volkswagen with a flower on the antenna. A woman's car. A not-Sandra woman.

Bob drove on.

Bob went to Bob's.

It was 11 a.m. and Bob wondered if it was too early for lunch. He decided not. He made himself a salmon-salad sandwich and took it and a bag of chips to the living room. Plate in lap, he turned on the TV and found a tennis match being played. Somewhere a tennis match was being played. The two combatants were foreigners with unpronounceable names that Bob had never heard before. It was diversion enough.

Afterward, Bob put his dish in the sink. He thought about rinsing it and putting it in the dishwasher but decided to forego that stage until later. For Bob this was sloppiness akin to leaving dirty underwear on the floor. He was trying to free himself from the merciless grip of assiduousness.

Bob went to his bedroom, in search of pornographic videos. Bob needed to pleasure himself. Depression had kept him from his duties and he was backed up. A warm insistence stirred in Bob's apparatus, a compression, a pulse in the scrotum. He found an appropriate tape—one he hadn't utilized in a while—and took it back to the living room. The light was pouring in through the windows like honey. Honey. It was a little too bright for such a private act, but Bob was beyond such consideration.

On screen, there was no preface to the action, no buildup. The scene opened on a naked couple, spread like gutted fowl on a cheesy bed, the bleach-blonde woman mouthing the oversized linga of an athletic stud. Bob opened his own shorts. His manhood was wee. Bob could only grip it with two fingers; there was no purchase.

Bob refocused his attention on the screen. Yes, that was erotic activity. Yes, it was quite exciting. Bob's button would not activate.

Argh, Bob thought. Distracted is what I am, Bob cogitated until he identified his hitch. Something was bothering Bob. Then he had it: the plate was still in the sink. Bob held his pants with one hand, shambled into the kitchen, took said plate in his one free hand and shoved it into the dishwasher.

Back in front of the TV, the couple had gone on without him. Our heroine now rode the stud in what Bob believed was called the Cowboy Position. Bob's libido awakened asudden. It was a nice session.

Afterward, Bob lay awash in his own fluid, pants at his ankles, TV back on tennis. Bob's mind drifted. He may have even drowsed. Without warning there came a knocking at the door. Bob arose as if he'd been caught doing something shameful. He stumbled, attempting to lift his trousers and make the door in one movement. The knocking continued.

"Wait," Bob said.

With some difficulty he managed to rebuckle his pants. He opened the door. It was Honey.

"Jesus," she said in greeting. "What were you doing?"

"What do you mean?" Bob asked.

Honey looked at Bob the way one might look at a dog which had tried to hump a hassock.

Bob switched gears. "What do you need?" he asked.

"Did I leave my camera here?" Honey asked, breezing by him.

It's my camera, thought Bob. But he said nothing. The sneaky guilt he felt, incongruously or not, made Bob meek. Even meeker than usual.

He could hear Honey rummaging around in the bedroom. Oh, God, Bob thought, I left the bag of videos on the bed. Shit, he thought. And his hand went to his lower stomach where there was a good-sized soggy patch. Honey was going to smirk at him. He didn't need that right now.

Honey emerged from the hallway, camera in hand. Her face was—it was—superior—and *smirk-ready*.

Bob started to speak before she could ridicule him.

Honey was too fast.

"You left a dirty plate in the sink," Honey said, as she headed for the door. "You're slipping," she said, parting.

"I don't understand," Rick said that night.

"Dammit, I'm haunted, spooked, visited by something from another realm."

"Because you forgot to put a dish in the dishwasher."

"I didn't—and the toothpaste cap. And the sage."

Rick barked an unintentional laugh.

"Bob, the *spices*?"

"Yes, they're always alphabetized, see. Always."

"Don't panic, buddy. You know what I think? Honey is messing with you."

Bob thought about this for a moment.

"The spice rack maybe. But she didn't sneak in and uncap the toothpaste. And—wait—see, she was the one who pointed out the dirty plate. Oh, wait, you think she took it out of the dishwasher? No, no, that's not right. She didn't know that I had just been bothered—that I had *just* put it away."

"So, what you're saying is something unseen is at work. Poltergeists that have nothing better to do than mess with your alphabetization."

"No, don't you see—what if this is actually how they get you—not rattling chains or footsteps in the attic or table knocking—but by small, seemingly insignificant *moves*—just a little each day to make you doubt your own volition—to make you aware of them."

"Okay, now you're creeping me out. That's—just, well, stupid."

"But it creeps you out."

"Okay, look, you wanna sleep at my house for a while? It would be cool. I think you're haunted all right, by loneliness. You're just not used to being alone."

"No, no—what about—who was at your house? You had a woman—"

"Yes, right. Kathy, Kathy Faulk."

"Kathy from high school?"

"Right."

"And Sandra—how did you—nevermind. How do you ever? You're—insatiable."

"B—"

"Sorry, that was unkind. I'm—jealous, I guess. Anyway— I'm all right alone. Really."

Bob went home that night feeling even more remote from sympathy, an alien to human compassion. Even his best friend who understood everything was distancing himself. Okay, it wasn't literally true—Bob was indulging in self-pity, relishing it really. Rolling around in isolation like a rooting swine. Bob was spooked into spiraling solipsism.

The house seemed hot, as hot as love's flaming climate. Bob was uncomfortable in his own skin—he itched. He rubbed at himself, wanting to strip away everything, everything that held him, clothed him, everything that made him Bob. He settled for pulling all his clothes off. He kicked pants, shirt, briefs into the air and let them fall where they would. He was sweating.

Bob Plumb turned around like a dog situating itself and looked frenetically about. His body felt prickly, yet alive— alive! He rubbed his hand over his oh-so-solid protoplasm— his arms, ribcage, his belly, thighs, crotch. Desire stirred momentarily. But onanism was not what Bob was seeking. What was it?

Bob lay down on the crappy carpet in his living room. The ceiling above him whirled like the souped-up heavens. The water spot in the corner resembled a head, in profile, speaking, its moist mouth permanently ajar.

And, as he lay there, Bob thought about his life, how wrong it had gone, how it was his fault partly, but not entirely. Some things had just happened, like they might happen to any man. As natural as a shower of rain.

It was then that Bob noticed his two pieces of wall art, reproductions in cheap frames. One was Chagall's "Bouquet with Flying Lovers." The other Larry Rivers' "Parts of the Body: French Vocabulary Lesson." Someone had moved them. The Chagall was where the Rivers used to be, and vice versa.

Bob considered the new placement of his prints. And he smiled.

Let's do a gentle fade here. We've gone with Bob about as far as we can go. His *ignis fatuus* is not our *ignis fatuus*. Each to his or her own phantoms, his or her own hauntings, and so on. Sleep well, Bob Plumb.

The Boy Who Used Up a Word

Timmy Erasmus Timmers was a kid. He was just an average kid. He liked basketball, video games, and meat-lover's pizzas. He liked Charlie Chaplin movies and *Encyclopedia Brown* books and The Beatles. He even liked his little sister, Annabeth.

So it was not any special, concealed, or secret magical power in the eleven-year-old that led to the strange occurrence that caused such a stir in Baileysville. And then beyond. Timmy would later say he was just messing around, experimenting. Not in the evil-scientist sense but in the kid-with-nothing-to-do-on-a-Saturday sense.

The truth is that Timmy Timmers used up a word. He had talked to his friend Ed "Jackpot" Burton at school that Friday about the possibility. Ed thought it was a keen idea and was anxious to help.

But Timmy wanted to do it himself.

His hypothesis was this: if he said a word enough times he would use it up. It would cease to exist, disappear even from the world's largest, unabridged dictionary. That was his working hypothesis. Simple enough, if you have the patience.

So, on Saturday, after calling a few friends to see if he could find a ball game or a companion to explore Bluefield Woods, and coming up empty, Timmy sat down to begin his experiment in earnest.

Picking the word was a problem, as Ed had predicted it would be.

"Pick something gross," Ed "Jackpot" Burton had said.

"No, I don't want to do gross," Timmy said, with a serious shake of his blond head.

"Pick a word your parents use a lot. That way when they get mad at you or something you can take away part of their ammunition."

"My parents don't get mad very often. And when they do they speak so calmly it really rattles your bones. They're not name-callers."

"Hm," Ed said.

Both boys appeared stumped.

So, Timmy decided to pick a word at random. A word he hoped was in common usage, one whose disappearance would be noticed. But he didn't want trouble.

He opened his *Webster*'s and stuck a finger down on the page. It was like picking a vacation spot by spinning the globe.

"Drakelet, a young drake," the dictionary said.

"Naw," Timmy said aloud.

He closed the heavy book and reopened it like a magician pulling a trick.

"Gruelly, having the consistency of gruel."

"No good," Timmy said. Maybe randomness was not the answer. He gave it one more try.

"Hey," he said. "This has possibilities."

He rolled the word around in his mouth. It was simple enough, brief enough. He could spend the day and night saying this word over and over easy enough.

At ten-thirteen that fateful Saturday morning, Timmy began.

He lay back against his pillows and began saying the word over and over.

He had no idea how many times he would have to say it. How would he know if he failed? He hadn't thought about that.

As the afternoon wore on he grew tired. Except for a break for a fried bologna sandwich for lunch he did not stop saying the word.

At dinner that evening he wolfed down his food.

"Eat slowly, dear," Timmy's mother said.

"I'll race you," said Annabeth.

"You got after-dinner plans?" Timmy's dad asked.

"No," Timmy said around a half-masticated piece of chicken.

"Don't talk with your mouth full," Timmy's mother said, smiling.

After dinner Timmy was hard at it again. His TV remained cold. His video paddles lifeless on the floor.

Around 10 p.m. his dad stuck his head in the door.

"Whatcha doing, son? Chanting?"

"No," Timmy said, anxious not to spend too much energy on unnecessary words.

"Okay. I thought I heard you talking in here. Listen, we're going to bed to read a while and then go to sleep. You don't stay up too late."

"Mm," Timmy said.

"Good night, then," his dad said, closing the door.

Around midnight Timmy's throat began to hurt. His neck felt tired as if he had carried something strapped around it. He was losing faith in his experiment.

Then it happened.

Sometime right around the change of dates Timmy found he could not say the word any longer. Was he just tired?

"Drakelet," he said.

No, he could still talk. He tried to remember the word. He could not. It was gone.

He went to his dictionary but he had no idea how to look up the word because the word was gone, not only from the dictionary but also from his head. And from the heads of the rest of the world.

At school on Monday, Timmy's teacher, Miss Parrish, called on Timmy to read from their lesson book, from the story about the headless horseman.

Timmy began to read but his voice was croaky.

"Are you okay?" Miss Parrish asked.

"Cold, maybe," Timmy rasped.

"Okay, Wendy Ceccherrelli, pick up where Timmy left off."

At breaktime Timmy couldn't wait to talk to Ed. He caught up with him in the hall and pulled him into the bathroom. There was a third grader in there but they didn't pay him any mind.

"I did it," Timmy whispered.

"You did? It worked?" Ed said. His pleasure was genuine.

"Took all day," Timmy said.

"What was the word," Ed said in his excitement.

"It's gone," Timmy said.

Ed thought a moment.

"Of course," he said. "Um, now what?"

"I don't know," Timmy whispered. "But the word's gone."

"You wanna do another?" Jackpot asked.

"Naw," Timmy said.

"Maybe I'll do one tonight."

"Maybe it's not such a good idea," Timmy whispered. It just occurred to him what the possibilities of this anti-creative force were.

"You did one," Ed said, sulking. "I want to try, too."

Timmy went home that night in a bit of a funk. He was sorry he had used the word up.

All over the world there were gaps and hesitations in people's speech. It was slight, almost unnoticeable.

"Oh, what's the word I want?" was heard over and over again.

Timmy didn't know any of that. But, he sensed it. He had made a hole in the world, in an important part of the world. He had made a perforation in language.

Timmy was very sorry this had ever started. And now, what if Ed did it and then told someone and they told someone and on and on.

Timmy called Ed on the phone.

"Please don't do it," Timmy said.

"Relish, relish, relish, relish, relish, relish, relish," Jackpot said.

"Why did you choose that word?" Timmy asked.

"I hate relish," Ed said. "Relish, relish, relish…"

Before going to bed Timmy wrote himself a note. It said, "Relish. Check fridge. Chopped pickle in a jar."

The next morning Timmy ran to the refrigerator and opened the door. He started pulling condiments out in a frenzy. His note now said only, "Check fridge. Chopped pickle in a jar."

"What are you doing, dear?" his mom, asked. "I'll make you breakfast."

"I'm looking for something." Timmy said.

"Well, what, dear?"

"I can't remember. But I'll know it when I see it," he said.

In the back of the fridge, behind a jar of old honey mustard, Timmy found what he wanted. He pulled it out into the fresh air as if he were pulling a rabbit out of a hat.

The jar of chopped pickles was there all right. But where its name was supposed to be was blank white space.

"What's this?" he asked his mom, frantic now.

Annabeth walked through the kitchen, her face smeared with syrup.

"Let's see," Mom said, sliding her reading glasses up her nose. "Well, dog my cats, there's no name on it. Ingredients: pickles, salt, water, spices. Hm."

"But what's it CALLED?" Timmy shouted.

Timmy's mom looked at him over her glasses, a silent reproach to his raising his voice.

"Well, I don't know what it is. To be safe I'm going to throw it away."

And she did. Out it went.

"Now, what would you like for breakfast?"

When Timmy got to school a red-eyed Ed met him on the front steps.

"Ha!" Ed said.

"Yeah," Timmy said.

"Hey, I was happy when you did it," Ed said.

NOTES TOWARD THE STORY AND OTHER STORIES

"I know. I'm sorry I did it though, Ed. You didn't tell anyone else did you?"

"Just Jackie and Jennie and Shlomo and Flannery and Garland and Pat and Sherri and Frank."

"Oh boy," Timmy said.

And that's how it all got started.

When the grammarians at Harvard University traced the trouble back to Baileysville, Timmy turned himself in.

"This is terrible," one of the grammarians said.

"I know," Timmy said. "I wish I could erase the whole thing. I wish I could go back in time and undo it."

"Not much chance of that," another grammarian said, a nice-looking lady with a "Just Read" button on her beige sweater.

"You've put us in quite a pickle, young man," said the man with the white beard who seemed to be in charge.

"Don't say 'pickle,'" Timmy said.

And so it happened. Little by little the language lost words, lost some very important words. Little by little writers lost the ability to create magic with the alphabet. It was a sad time for the planet.

World leaders went on television to plead with people to stop using up words but the more they gave away the secret the more people tried it. It was irresistible. It was quickly out of control.

And it wasn't just in English this was happening. All over the globe people were using up words just because they could. In Swahili, in French, in Italian, in German, in Polish, in Hmong.

Writers were in despair. Some stopped writing.

The production of books dropped 8 percent the first year. The next year it was down 17 percent.

No one knew what to do.

But a lesson was learned. Even as it trickled away, like sands through an hourglass, language took on a new significance. People began to appreciate the words that were left.

Yet still they ebbed away. There was no turning back.

Stories, the ones that were still written, and the ones already written, began to have holes in their sentences. The opening of *A Tale of Two Cities* now read, "It was the best of times, it was the of times." No one knew what went in the cavity.

Some people stopped reading. It was too difficult.

It was a nightmare.

I know. I'm a writer. I put this down on paper as a for all of us.

Notes Toward the Story

"Every story is not about some question.
Yes it is. Where all is known no narrative is possible."

—Cormac McCarthy

→Possible opening of story:

They were loud and ill-mannered, but hell, so was I at their age. We had just moved to the neighborhood and I didn't want to start right away being the old grouch all the kids loved to hate. It worried me a bit when Chip was around, but they seemed relatively harmless.

Chip was my five-year-old; Chip as in "off the old block," but I was not trying to forge him in my image, God knows, you'll have to believe me on that.

*

Drawcansir—a blustering big bully.

*

Chip's note to my new wife:
　　Kiss me n the morning
　　be a surpriz

*

Chip's idea for a novel: Beowulf II—story of Grendel's father

*

There's a knife, an ordinary kitchen knife, which I cannot look at. When my wife leaves it on the counter I see it as an invitation to mayhem or suicide. What's beneath flesh beckons. The knife has an inner life.
Also: we have a ricer. I do not know what a ricer is. Do I need to know this?

*

Dogs don't understand sarcasm. Go ahead. Tell your dog who has just shit on the welcome mat, Yeah, that's what I want you to do. The dog will offer you unbreakable insouciance.

*

Was this some kind of test, a trust exam after all this time? Was it some stratagem designed to discover the real me, a me that was hidden, or worse, a me that existed unbeknownst to me, a

Hyde-me, an ur-me, a newand-improved me that would delight her, or a hideous monster-me that would disappoint, abandon, maim?

*

And now, stretching toward the horizon, there are two shadows.

*

My wife has no idea about Brier. Brier, my nineteen-year-old lover.
Brier.
The medicine you're taking is making you sick.

*

Trepanning—drilling a hole in the skull for a permanent high

*

"Things are slow, here at The Doterage."

*

Pudency (PYOOD-n-see) adjective
Modesty, bashfulness.
If today's word bears a resemblance to the word for female privates,
it's

because there is a link. Both sprout from Latin *pudere* (to be ashamed).
Impudent is another word originating from the same source.

*

Chip walks in while I'm on the phone with Brier. He hears this: "and that's because I have developed an overwhelming urge and overwhelming urges are as unavoidable as allegory." Later, Chip will ask me what an allegory is. He will ask me what an overwhelming urge is. He will ask me, Who is Brier?

*

Rubicon—point of no return, where an action taken commits a person irrevocably

*

→Chip's father is trying to start a new story. In truth I am trying to start a new novel by starting a new story that will take hold like an infection and become a year's work. A novel.

*

Sciolist—one who engages in pretentious display of superficial knowledge

*

Chip's thoughts on non-representational art, after looking at Faith Ringgold's work: "Oh, it's like Claude Monet, whose pictures are kind of floppy."

*

Impressionism, even at its best, is kind of floppy. Yes.

*

(Doterage. Funny?)

A knife. A ricer.

*

The boys, the boys in my imaginary neighborhood, form a loose gang. We do not think it's gang as in gang warfare, as in gangland, as in gang-related-shooting. These boys are from good homes, bright boys, even happy boys. Together, the groupthink takes over, as groupthink must. They become something slightly more dangerous. I use the word advisedly. They are boys like my boy—yet, they are contemplating something outré, something hideous.

*

What?

Furphy—a false story, a rumor

*

Potemkin village (po-TEM-kin VIL-ij) noun
  An impressive showy facade designed to mask undesirable facts.

*

Call the street we live on—the street the imaginary we live on—Potemkin Street?

*

My wife—my new wife, as we all refer to her—is named Hayley. Like Hayley Mills, whose underwear, once glimpsed as a child in *The Parent Trap*, set up inside the young me inexplicable detonations and collisions which later would produce, or help produce, an adult who is led around by his dick. Hayley Mills' Underpants.

*

Brier says this: "Look, you're married. That's fine. I knew you were married. Your being married is one of your chief definitions. It is, perhaps, one of the things that drew me to you. And together, you and I, we, appositives acceptable, have great sex, and having had great sex, we whisper endearments that we both mean and do not mean. We are in a nether world. We are in a temporary way station, a waiting room. But, having agreed upon that, there is no reason why we, in our way station, cannot continue to fuck like squirrels and enjoy the pleasures given to so few humans in this makeshift world."

*

Brier talks like this. She is, as they say, wise beyond her years. And she has a tattoo of a rose on the left cheek of her perfect ass. This rose is a Rubicon.

*

The boys broke into Mr. Thompson's shed and stole his riding lawnmower. They took it for a joyride. They left Mr. Thompson's riding lawnmower in the culvert at the end of Potemkin Street.
Taking a riding lawnmower for a joyride seems funny to me. Would it seem funny to readers, strangers? Is funny the way I want this story to go? Can it be both funny and tragic and if so how?

*

Resistentialism (ri-zis-TEN-shul-iz-um) noun
    The theory that inanimate objects demonstrate hostile behavior
against us.

*

Gadzookery—use of archaic words.

*

Hayley says this at dinner: "Who is Brier?"

*

Polyvalent—multifaceted, having many layers.

Chip says this to me Saturday morning: "Why is Mommy crying?"

*

I tell Chip, my son, this: "Mommy and Daddy have had a little misunderstanding. It's nothing to worry about. We will, as we always do, work things out."

*

→The boys, after numerous backyard break-ins, broken gate locks, lawnmowers stolen, resold, dismantled, pushed into ditches, swapped with neighbors' lawnmowers, progress to larger misdeeds. Firstly, they torture Mrs. Pewitt's dog and set it on fire. Dogs don't understand fire any better than they understand sarcasm. The dog lives and walks the neighborhood, a blackened, limping thing, a caution sign. A warning like a black rose.
The boys then pick on a smaller boy. A bad something begins to grow, a malefaction.
Chip.
(The boys sexually harass Hayley?)

*

Hayley says this: "What were you thinking? What were you thinking? What were you thinking?"

*

Grivoiserie: bold licentious behavior.

*

Chip says this: "When you write your face goes funny"
How funny, I ask him.
Mean. Chip says, Your face goes mean.

*

Can I sacrifice my only begotten son to the mob? Can I do it for the sake of Story? Can I do it as expiation for my sins? Is a writer not like God?

*

Excerebrose (eks-SER-ee-bros) adjective
Brainless.

*

Brier says this: "Let me sit on you. I like it when you watch me. I like to be on top of you. Big man. My big man. Yes yes yes yes."

*

Zoophyte—an animal resembling a plant.

*

The shooting has "gang overtones," Sgt. Melendez said. Neighbors in the area said they were shocked that the shooting could happen in their quiet neighborhood near Grahamwood Elementary School. At the time there were at least four children near the house on Potemkin. One small girl was in the front yard. The bullets were flying over her head, Sgt. Melendez said. "Gang overtones," he reiterated. "Gang overtones." The neighborhood took up the phrase like a chant, a spell.

Chip was supposed to be playing with those children. Instead he was inside the house, a headache sidelining his weekend plans.

*

Chip says this to Hayley: "You're more beautiful than Halle Berry." Halle Berry, for whatever reason, has become Chip's measure for earthly beauty.

*

Man to wife after affair is discovered: I got excited, okay? I got excited. Me. The dead, desiccated husk of a formerly vibrant man, your husband, got excited.

*

Hayley says this to Chip: "You are my shining star, my knight errant."

*

Brier says this: "You bastard. You're a bastard. Of course your wife knows. I told you this would happen. I told you so many times. Shit, you know what, I don't care. Listen. Listen, you bastard, I'm still here. Okay? I don't care. We can still fuck whenever one or both of us feels like it. This is the way I live my life, Okay?"

*

Hayley stays with her husband.

*

The knife is out. It is always out. Knives are.

*

Chip becomes a young man of preternatural kindness and intuition.

*

The boys are arrested but not by Sgt. Melendez. They are all sent to "homes." The word "homes" as a euphemism began when? Potemkin Street went back to the peaceful oasis it had formerly been. A safe neighborhood. Whatever that means.

Chip spends most of his waking hours outside. We do not ask him what he does.

*

Hayley says this: "What were you thinking? What were you thinking? What were you thinking?"

*

Wamble (WOM-buhl) verb intr.
 1. To move unsteadily; to totter, waver, roll, etc.
 2. To feel nausea.
  3. (Of a stomach) To rumble or growl.
noun
 1. An unsteady motion.
 2. A feeling of nausea.

*

→Hayley is my new wife. She is beautiful the way new things are beautiful, cars, tools, affairs. When they made her they broke the mold (possible love interest in future for new teacher at the community college). Chip, as in "off the block," is my son, my only son, a good boy, as far as it goes. Brier is a visual artist. She calls herself a "visual artist." She will never marry. She will live in New York City for a while running a gallery her parents buy her (later self-destructive, or is that too radical a change?). (Suicide attempt? With knife? No.) Writer never sees lover again. (He does see her, [the monster-me?] every month or so, running into her at Whole Foods, or the video store, and they fuck, quickly, furtively, like teenagers who only know they must, and never consider consequences. Who must get it over with quickly.) (Writer grows ill—venereal? Too out-of-date? Obsolete? Gout?) (Writer never finishes book. Someone else usurps the urban gang theme and writes a bestseller?) (Writer visits New York, finds gallery—what happens?) (Hayley asks for a divorce years later, years later?) (Hayley declares love for English teacher, another writer?) (Chip—into drugs?) (The dog's name?)

What next? What next? What next?

Mike and Doris Had Everything

Mike and Doris had everything. The home the newlyweds had chosen was a steal, especially in the neighborhood where they found it. And it was stuffed with all the accouterment of modern living, including many entertainment devices currently available.

On one blithe Saturday morning Doris leaned back, hands behind her pretty head, and said aloud, "We have everything." She smiled at her handsome husband, standing before her in serviceable bathrobe and slippers.

Mike grinned like a possum.

A small cloud spit in Doris's eye. "Don't we?" she demanded.

"Everything except a sugar bowl," Mike said, still grinning.

"Is that an expression?" Doris asked, a small choke to her voice.

"No. Literally, we don't have a sugar bowl."

"Didn't one of your cousins—the gay one in Michigan—"

"Creamer."

161

"Oh," Doris squeaked. Her brow tightened like a bowstring. She now thought she was going to have a good long cry, the like of which Mike had never seen.

"Jesus, honey," Mike said. "I was being breezy. I'll get dressed right now and go get us a sugar bowl."

On his way out the door Doris called from somewhere in the house, "Make it a nice one."

Mike drove to Pottery Barn, a few miles away in a tony strip mall.

As he parked the car a dark, lovely woman in a midriff blouse was getting out of an adjacent vehicle. Mike was a sucker for midriff blouses.

And she smiled.

"Your midsection is like mead by the warm breezes fanned," Mike offered. "I cannot continue to breathe if I don't place my cheek there."

When Mike came home later that day Doris was out. Whit Whitaker, her old boyfriend from high school had called, and she couldn't resist one more highly charged fuck, Whit Whitaker was just that attractive.

Shadow Work

"Taking it in its deepest sense, the shadow is the invisible saurian tail that man still drags behind him. Carefully amputated, it becomes the healing serpent of the mysteries. Only monkeys parade with it."

—Carl Jung

Some say it started in Europe, like existentialism and psychotherapy. The truth is, however, that it was probably, initially, an American innovation because its contours were American: its swank exclusivity, its decadent solipsism. In the major metropolitan areas, New York City, Los Angeles, Chicago, Boston, it spread so quickly that it was as if it had always existed. In a matter of months, they were seen everywhere, in bright daylight on urban sidewalks, a vaporous dayglow, or evenings cast against grayish backgrounds by gentle streetlight or moon. Moonshadows were especially pleasing.

For Valerie, the issue was not whether she would have her shadow dyed—that was, as the young say, a no-brainer—it was whether to tell her twin, Vicki, about her plans. She and Vicki were close, don't get that wrong. And, being identical twins, the issue partly became whether their shadows should also be identical. They were not the sort of identical twins who dressed alike. If Valerie opted for the magenta with iridescent gold highlights, which is what she was leaning toward, should Vicki then do likewise? Or, and here Valerie really balked as if reprimanded, should she consult with her twin before even scheduling the session? What if Vicki wanted the anodized purple? Or, gad, the new tie-dye?

In Memphis, where trends arrived on the last coach, there were already three parlors specializing in dyed shadows, two of which were also tattoo parlors (where the option had become *le dernier cri*, quickly) and one was a freestanding business in what used to be a 7/11: P. Cocky's. The tattoo parlors, Peter Pan's and Midtown Colours (they insisted on the superfluous "u" because it sounded *European*), were having a price war. P. Cocky's was a more elegant establishment and kept mum through the whole Shadow Color Wars. They were the tony top dog. Their reputation, already, was so solid that they did not feel the need to compete.

So, it was to P. Cocky's that Valerie went one day, the money in her purse hard earned at her job as a mall security officer. She stood uncertainly in the doorway. The walls were papered with bright, blown-up photographs of happy people, trailed by shadows of every imaginable hue. The shadows, in the photos, seemed super-real, magnified, and overly bright. The shadows Valerie had seen in real life were slightly plainer, though grand in their way. Some people swore their dyed shadows had changed their lives, made them more confident, in their relationships, in their business dealings. Some said it was as if they were trailing light itself, instead of its obverse. Shadow envy was, suddenly, a bona fide social phenomenon. Valerie, still fighting inwardly with her devotion to her sister, left the shop, after picking up one of their eye-catching brochures.

The reason Valerie wanted the somewhat-expensive procedure was the old story: she wanted to gain a young man's attention. The young man in question was named Tommy "Dago" Swell. He had gone to the same high school as the twins and had been the school's starting point guard on a team that went all the way to State. Coach Handbag said Dago was the best point guard he had coached since "Tiny" Barthelme. Dago was lean and muscular and wore his hair gassed straight back from his forehead. His tattoos were legendary, vistas previously unknown to the eyes of men. And Dago Swell was the first student at Ransom P. Stoddard High School to get his shadow done—it was a small scandal since shadow dyeing was an adults-only procedure at the time. But, because Dago looked eighteen when he was fifteen and twenty-five when he was seventeen, he passed easily. When he first came to school, highlighted, nonchalance belying a secret pride, his shadow was itself shadowed by a gaggle of underclassmen who had already worshiped Dago Swell as an athlete and now could revere him as a god. On the basketball court the varicolored shadow caused other problems. Occasionally flickering into view, a polychrome glint in peripheral vision, it was responsible for the team's increased steals record. But opposing players were afraid to point a finger, such was Dago's spiky reputation.

Valerie thought Dago just about the hottest male she had ever encountered. She thought he was the cats. She had been in love with him since ninth grade, and when he got a job as a security guard at the mall alongside her she was fit to be tied. It had been assumed that Dago would attend the University of Memphis on a basketball scholarship but his grades were poor and, when it was suggested he go to junior college first, he gave up basketball, just like that. If his reputation suffered because of his change from baller to rent-a-cop, you couldn't tell it by Valerie. She still thought he was as sexy as a winter pear, one she longed to take a bite out of.

Vicki knew of her sister's moderate betrayal. Her twin ESP was more fully developed than Valerie's, to the point that Vicki occasionally listened in on her sister's private conversations simply by tilting her head toward the north and shutting one eye halfway. She heard Valerie tell her friend, Elspeth, that she had saved enough for a dye and was contemplating not telling Vicki. Elspeth answered with her own terse eloquence: "Whatever." Elspeth put herself above many of the world's more mundane proceedings. She feigned that she had seen it all. Vicki's own secret was that she was in love with Elspeth.

"Oh, you've had your shadow done," Valerie said the first day Dago came to work.

Dago gave her the look he reserved for boiled codfish.

"Years ago," he said, his fingers playing over his nightstick.

Valerie's face burned with shame. What a stupid thing to say! Did he know her? Did he realize that she was at Ransom P. Stoddard with him and hence would know before now about his infamous shadow? She wanted to die.

"I'm Valerie," she said.

Dago Swell looked into the middle distance. There he seemed to find a more interesting tête-à-tête and he slowly moved away, trailing behind him a candent bismuth-yellow-and-viridian eidolon. Valerie shrank. She became wee. She almost disappeared.

The next day Valerie returned to P. Cocky's with a fresh resolve. She didn't have to go to work until 8 p.m., and she was determined to show up with a brightly hued shadow, one that would knock Dago Swell out of his high-tops. Her sister Vicki sat in their bedroom, the one they had shared since they were born, and tuned into her sister's erratic aura. It was flickering like a wounded thing and it was all Vicki could do to regulate its message. When she did she realized the degree of Valerie's disloyalty and she felt cheerless. She felt jilted and forsaken. She picked up the phone and dialed Elspeth's number.

"It's Vicki," Vicki said. "Valerie's sister."

"I know."

"What are you doing?" Vicki didn't know how to woo. That was clear.

"Hmph."

"Wanna—" and here Vicki drew a blank. What did she want to ask of Elspeth? To go get coffee? To catch a movie? She was suddenly up against it. Dating—it was a foreign concept.

"Where's Valerie?" Elspeth asked in the lacuna between words.

"She's—" Vicki burst into tears.

Elspeth waited a few moments and then, calmly, hung up.

Vicki dried her eyes. After letting the sobs dissipate she decided that she had done okay for a first foray. She felt that she was on the righteous road to romance.

Meanwhile, Valerie was in the backroom of P. Cocky's, prone in their elegant leather chair, which looked like something between a barber's and a masseuse's. The dyer was a middle-aged man with a ponytail and only one tattoo, but that one tattoo was in the middle of his forehead and was an eye. "My pineal," he said. The dyer's name was Rip.

"Relax," Rip said. "It only hurts for a second. You wanna smoke to calm you down?"

"Grass?" Valerie asked, squinching her face.

"Uh, no, that would be illegal," Rip said, but he didn't offer an alternative.

"No thanks," Valerie said. She couldn't stop her feet from dancing.

"Okay," Rip said. "Away we go."

When she got home that afternoon, Valerie felt a little nauseous. She sat in her car, in her parents' driveway, willing her stomach to go easy on her. After a few minutes she felt a little better. When she stepped from the car she saw it for the first time. Rip had said that the process takes anywhere from a half-hour to an hour to take effect. So, emerging from her Toyota into the full blast of afternoon daylight, Valerie was able to behold the enormous change in her incorporeal self for the first time. She stepped away from the car. The shadow sprung out in front of her like a red carpet. Except it wasn't red. It was cobalt violet. With gold highlights! She had asked for magenta but Rip had talked her out of it. "Magenta—it's for tourists, tourists and receptionists. Not a serious color for shadows. I recommend the much subtler cobalt violet."

"Okay," Valerie said. "Can I still have gold highlights?"

Now, Valerie looked at her gold highlights. She loved her gold highlights! She twirled in the driveway like a child with a new dress. The air was ripe with spring and Valerie was a kaleidoscope. Valerie was a dappled fairy castle! She spun until she was dizzy.

Vicki stood in the carport doorway behind the screen door. She watched her sister's self-centered dance. Vicki felt the tears coming again. But, she did not cry. Gradually, like the slow glow of an ember, Vicki began to feel extraordinarily happy. Her sister was beautiful. Valerie was like a glittery butterfly just emerged from her dun cocoon. A smile grew on Vicki's face, a smile that made the plain girl suddenly quite lovely.

Valerie stopped her caper and leaned against the Toyota for support. Then she saw Vicki behind the screen door and her heart stopped. Guilt flooded her. And Vicki, behind that metal scrim, looked as if she was installed in a black-and-white movie. Her silhouette was positively colorless, gray like a shallow sea. Valerie felt heartsick. And she knew she had to face her sister and tell her loving things and cuddle her and convince her that she too needed the dye job. She would tell Vicki that the only reason she did this was to be a guinea pig for the two of them. She wanted to show her sister that this was a selfless act, an act of bravery designed to brighten their lives. That was her tack. That was what she knew she must do.

But when she entered their home Vicki threw her arms around her sister and wept onto her shoulder.

"I'm so sorry," Valerie said.

"No," Vicki said, still snuffling into her neck. "You are the most beautiful thing I've ever seen."

"Oh, Vicki!" Valerie said. "Oh, my sister!"

"And Dago Swell is gonna eat you like cake," Vicki said.

That stopped the love fest for a moment. How did Vicki know the secret of her twin's heart of hearts, the one secret

Valerie held dearest? It was twin ESP, of course, Valerie realized; it was not the first time it had occurred between them. Vicki was fine-tuned. She was powerful.

The rest of the afternoon, the twins stayed in their room, casting Valerie's new shadow against each and every surface with the dazzling light from a gooseneck lamp. When their mother called them to the dinner table the twins emerged, their arms locked, exchanging small kisses, petting each other as if they were new lovers. Their mother paused as she passed around the hamburger hash. Something was new. Something about her beloved daughters was brand new—and, somehow, as exciting as a spiritual awakening!

Valerie insisted Vicki go to the mall with her that evening. She didn't want to part from her twin now, now that their bond was reestablished. Really, it was such a slight thing, their rift, so easily repaired.

"You can go to Gap while we're there. I'll buy you something," Valerie said.

Vicki could only smile at her generous sister. Such love. On the way to the mall Valerie asked Vicki if she had thought about dyeing her shadow.

"It's really a good time to do it," she suggested. "Before, you know, everyone makes it trashy."

"If it's gonna be trashy, why do it?" Vicki countered, but with a smile.

"Well, the way I see it, we have the opportunity of being forerunners, and by making it beautiful *now*, we sort of set the ground rules, the groundwork, you know."

"I'll think about it," Vicki said. "Should we match?"

"Yes!" Valerie said. "Let's match!"

The twins entered the mall as if they were royalty come down into their kingdom for a visit, for a tour of all they governed. They shopped. They spent good money on good clothes and gaudy baubles. They were happy.

Vicki followed Valerie to work. There they ran into Dago Swell, who was just coming off duty. His uniform hugged him like a second skin. His nightstick was a dark dream-symbol.

"Hey Dago," Valerie said. She was showing her sister how easygoing it all was, this Dago thing. How blithe it was.

Dago Swell looked at the twins as if they were circus freaks, as if they were two-headed or had snake scales. Had he really never noticed them before, at Ransom P. Stoddard High? Perhaps not. He walked on clouds.

"Twins," he said, as if the word was a naming he could be proud of.

Vicki laughed. Valerie burned red, looked at her sister as if she had just burped in church.

"We're not twins," Vicki said, simpering. "We are the same person but occasionally it is called upon us—me—to travel to two places at once. It's a secret, so don't tell."

Dago Swell looked at this new girl, this mirror image of Valerie, Valerie—whom he had already dismissed in his mind, in his heart. She was an echo of her less interesting sister, a capricious echo.

"You got a mouth on you," Dago Swell said. "You giving me lip?"

Vicki smiled. Flirting with a man was easy because she had no emotional investment in it. It was sport. She looked at Valerie, and Valerie's stricken expression was like a tuning fork in her head. Yet Vicki found that betraying her sister was as uncomplicated a trick as a conjurer swallowing a poker. She uncovered a part of herself previously unidentified.

"You look like you could use some lip," Vicki said.

The air, the sweet mall air, crackled.

"I'm off work now," Dago Swell said. "You come have coffee with me. You want to come have coffee with me?"

Vicki allowed herself one quick glance at Valerie. Then she switched off her ESP and left the mall with Dago Swell.

Valerie burst into tears. And she cried the whole time she walked the mall that night. Before the place closed many salespeople saw the crying cop pass and they shook their heads at the slight alteration in their otherwise tedious night selling perfume or books or pretzels or sex toys.

"Did you see the cop crying?"

"I did. Female cop, too."

"Yeah."

"Did you notice her shadow?"

"I didn't. She have her shadow done? Maybe that's why she's crying. I'm telling you that's messing with something that shouldn't be messed with, you know? Like DNA or something. That shadow work is tricky stuff. Hell, it made her cry."

And that was what the story became: the fable of a girl whose shadow job messed up her hormonal balance. That particular take on things caught on. It became, gradually, the truth.

All that night, after the mall closed, Valerie walked her rounds, sobbing, her colorful shadow trailing her like a spurned bride's train. The colors failed to glow. The shadow was inert, all but useless.

The next morning the breakfast table at Vicki and Valerie's house was a place of inaudibly festering loneliness. Mother and Father ate alone, neither feeling it incumbent upon them to discuss their absent twins. The truth was that Valerie, alone, was in the bedroom. After coming in at 4:35

a.m., and seeing that Vicki had not come home at all, Valerie renewed her seemingly endless torrent of tears and never did collapse gratefully into the arms of Morpheus. After 8:30 a.m., when she was sure both her parents had departed, she dragged herself to the kitchen, fixed an indifferent cup of coffee, accompanied by a stale sticky bun, and sat with both in front of her and ate not and drank not and let the morning sun, coming in the window, smear her face and make tiny rainbows of her tears and she let the warmth enter her like a flu and she cursed her shadow and she cursed Dago Swell and, most of all, she cursed her foul, perfidious sister.

Vicki came home sometime later. She was chipper. She was animated. She was like a fresh apple, juicy and bright and full of sin. Valerie put on a brave face. That's what they call it: a brave face.

"Good morning, Sis," Vicki said, rummaging in the refrigerator. "Whatchoo eating?"

"Bun," Valerie said. She felt perhaps single-syllable words would be okay.

"Where the hell is my kefir?" Vicki said.

Valerie concentrated on her coffee. If she took half-sips it would last twice as long.

Vicki sat with a cup of coffee and a box of shortbread cookies. She smiled at Valerie.

"Where?" Valerie said.

"Where was I?" Vicki stalled. "Well...first, no, not first. Here."

Vicki stood and placed herself against the light coming in the window. A versicolored shadow spilled over the breakfast table and onto Valerie's lap. It was shimmering like a trout freshly hooked. It did not match Valerie's at all. Worse, it outshone it. It was a deluxe job, with anodized mauve streaks.

Valerie thought she was going to be sick. The shadow on her lap felt like glistening poison, as if it were leaking into her.

"Do you like it?' Vicki asked.

"How," Valerie tried. A beat or two of attenuated time stretched between the twins.

"How could you?" Valerie finished and then leapt from her seat and disappeared.

Vicki stood in the kitchen sunlight for a while, sipping her coffee and admiring her own dodgy shadow. It was a threshold day, a day when things formerly one way became forever another. Vicki decided she was pleased that it was so.

Meanwhile, all over the planet Shadow Work became a hotly debated craze. Newer and more complex ways to dye shadows were invented practically daily. Some people, dragging around old unihued shadows, were suddenly cast as out of step, as if they were still watching Beta VCRs, or wearing the fashions of the year before. And, naturally, there sprang up movements which depicted Colored Shadows as dangerous, as corrupt. One such movement was called Daltonism and its followers were as fanatical as Green Peace zealots, though, honestly, they did not have that kind of moral weight behind them. Daltonists sprang up in every city, their meetings marked by a lot of bloviating and speechifying and much fun was poked at the Vainglorious Colored Shadow People. In Memphis a small chapter surfaced, meeting in the basement of First Congo Church. Enthusiasm didn't run very deep, however, and, after a few halfhearted gatherings, the group dissolved.

And so the twins grew apart. Where did the love go? The continental drift between them became cold and hard. They each thought the other a quisling.

"I don't know," Valerie lamented to Elspeth. "I think he's bad for her."

"Yah," Elspeth yawned. "But he'd a been good for you."

"No, I see that now," Valerie said. "I see how treacherous and shallow he is."

"Dago Swell is a piece of work," Elspeth said. Valerie didn't know if he was being praised or damned.

"Besides," Elspeth said. "I figured your sister for gay."

This gave Valerie pause.

"Why would you think that?" she asked.

"I thought she had the, you know, hots for me."

"You think everyone has the hots for you."

In a more conventional friendship this may have caused a serious breach.

"Yeah," Elspeth answered.

Time passed. Shadow Work became a part of the everyday. That is to say it was amalgamated into the warp and woof of dailiness and, if thought about at all, it was with the attention afforded haircuts or spring wardrobes. Some people had shadows that were prettier than other people's shadows. Some people still had charcoal-gray shadows, things which sometimes seemed quaint and sometimes seemed as beautiful as one of Durer's engravings. A new appreciation was born for some of the old ways and many saw this as a good thing.

Meanwhile, the twins were so estranged that they rarely spoke. Vicki and Dago Swell got a place of their own and Valerie quit her job at the mall—how could she do otherwise? She couldn't abide seeing Dago every day—and began working for a small private detective agency: Alec "Fast" Lemon's Shadow Bureau. It was mostly repo work, or adultery cases. Valerie hated it. She grew morose and waspish. Her shadow, once a glorious appendage, seemed to fade and achromatize. She dragged it behind her like a tattered bathrobe. She probably shouldn't have been issued a gun, but she was. It was all perfectly legal.

Vicki saw it coming. She was watching TV, eating Cheetos. Dago was asleep in the back room because lately he had been working the night shift. There was a tempering of the light, something at the edge of vision. At first Vicki thought it was just an anomaly of the TV reception. A sputter in her tangential vision. Then she realized that her shadow was bending unnaturally. It was moving, ever so slightly, *toward* the light. Her ears pricked, or perhaps her thumbs. She stood up just before she heard the shot.

In the back room Dago Swell lay face-down on the bed, a small, black puncture, deep as night, right in the center of his finespun foulard pajama top. Valerie stood at the foot of the bed, her face blank, her shadow a snapping shower of sparks. The room was unnaturally still as if the report of the gun had created a vacuum of silence and immobility. Very slowly, a shy creature emerging from its hole in the ground, a thick cord of bright red blood, surfaced from Dago's new opening.

Vicki quietly moved near her sister. She took her hand. The twins stood over the murdered body of Dago Swell and they held hands as if, against the indifference and gravity and approbation of the world, their united love was a safeguard, was ballast. And their shadows, their troublesome shadows, merged into one, pooling behind them on the hardwood floor, a colorful figuration, in fathomless hues like the wake of the helmsman's bark of yore, a final, vivid umbra.

Publisher

"That was commonly believed to be a function of great literature: antidote to suffering through depiction of our common fate."

—Philip Roth

1

I am a whore and a pimp. This may seem preposterous to you, but I assure you, though self-knowledge has not always been my strong suit, here I am neither exaggerating for shock value nor confessing for pity.

I came from good schools with a lot riding on me, the aspirations of my own ambition, duly inflated by well-intentioned professors and administrators, the hopes and dreams of my hardworking but underachieving parents, the burnout of my older brother, who was both smarter and more industrious. These are onerous pressures, each, and, collectively, quite oppressive. I was promise and capacity. I was Golden Boy. It was assumed I would make it, in the vague sense that expression is intended, but mostly this: procure a big bundle of money while doing meritorious things.

Oh, I started out with high hopes. With my degree in English lit tucked, metaphorically, under my arm (my area of specialty was Twentieth Century British Literature) I headed to New York City—where else?—with the aim of landing a job in publishing, figuring, naively, on walking into an assistant editorship at Knopf or Henry Holt or Farrar, Straus & Giroux. Figuring, I guess, they were hungry for a bright young man who had digested a lot of writing and practically passed metaphors and similes with his flatulence. You've guessed by my tone by now that the doors were not exactly swinging open for me. Oh, everyone was nice enough—egad, those publishing houses are filled with beautiful young twenty-four-year-old women fresh from college, firm jawed, severe, the kind of women who look you right in the eye until you look away no matter how unchallenging your last remark was—and I even had a few promising interviews. I actually met Roger Giroux—he must be 104—though it was in the corridor of the building where FS&G resides, and our conversation was brief, chatty, meaningless. He was, at that particular moment, concerned about some television show that had just aired (I gathered from his somewhat disjointed commentary) and which offended him deeply by its depiction of J. D. Salinger as a nasty old man. To be honest I'm not sure Mr. Giroux knew to whom he was talking or ever registered a single comment I made.

So, to pay the rent for my pitiable one-room apartment (New Yorkers settle for so little in the way of comfort, the city itself, supposedly, redressing the imbalance by its sizzle) I took up a job—where else?—in a bookstore in the Village, a squatty, dark, dank little dungeon where used books mixed with a random, arbitrary sampling of some of the newer offerings by our contemporary geniuses. If this all sounds rather bitter, rather sour-grape flavored, I plead guilty. I enjoyed spending my time in the bookstore—more often than not rearranging Trollope, Iris Murdoch, the Powyses or John Fowles, *ad infinitum,* one week alphabetizing their subsections by title, one week placing the books chronologically. And, if this was just idle make-work, the owner, Pat Trevelyn, a corpulent, ex-hippie who only wanted to make enough money to feed his cat and keep himself in marijuana, never questioned a single move I made. Nor did he recognize any of them.

So, the time went by, weeks and months. New York became a heavy yoke around my neck and my letters back home were full of book-talk, most of which I garnered from the eccentric clientele who frequented The Book Inglenook (a clumsy appellative which one can only imagine was designed to avoid the clichéd Book Nook) or from the sagacious pages of *The New York Times Book Review* and *The New York Review of Books*. It didn't take too many Ramen Noodle meals to make me realize what a failure I was, and I was on the verge of bailing out—running back to Saskatoon with my paper-stuffed suitcase—when an ad in the back of the *NYTBR* caught my attention.

It said: *Editor wanted. Small press. Benefits. Rapid advancement.* And a phone number.

I called—of course I called—and got the ubiquitous answering machine, and it wasn't until the next day when I returned home from the BI that a return message lit up the red-eye on my own machine. Its message, delivered in a smooth, slightly nasal but very proper voice said, "Mr. Brackett, thank you for answering our ad. If you could appear at our offices tomorrow morning at 9 a.m. we could talk further about this employment opportunity. Please bring a current resume." And he gave the address. An address which I was unfamiliar with, though I knew it was squirreled away among some claustrophobic uptown nondescript buildings, and, indeed, it turned out to be absurdly difficult to find. One had to wend one's way through trash-strewn alleyways, up some unpromising exterior stairways, down some darkened corridors, to finally arrive. I expected the Minotaur at any moment. It was almost as if it were consciously concealed.

The small white sign with black lettering on the door said, "Ardent Publishing, James Quillmeier, Publisher."

I gave the hollow plywood door a light knock while opening it enough to poke my head in. My first sight was a wall decorated entirely with oversize blow-ups of book jackets, presumably some of the firm's successes (though I had heard of none of them). Rotating my head a few degrees east I found a smiling visage, bright as a blister. It seemed to single-handedly hold back the room's fuscous gloom. The face belonged, it turned out, to Ardent's loyal secretary, Sherri Hoving, and it was a face which was to turn up in my dreams for years to come, a face like an iceberg refracting light, with a gaze like a baby uses on another baby. She was a brunette with skin like sealskin and she seemed to be both dark and light simultaneously. But, before I get ahead of the story, before I wax idyllic and burn my candle at both ends, leaving little suspense for your delectation, allow me to proceed into the cluttered and claustrophobic offices of Ardent Publishing.

"Mr. Brackett?" the face tinkled.

"Yes, I have..."

"Yes, I know. Mr. Quillmeier is expecting you. At the moment he is on the phone to Tokyo but he'll be with you momentarily, I'm sure."

"Thank you," I said and backed, self-consciously, into an old-fashioned armchair that was shoved against one wall.

The face beamed at me. I tried to beam back but my smile felt phony and I imagined I might have looked like Dr. Sardonicus. I tried to relax.

"Can I get you anything?" she asked after a few sunny moments.

"Nothing, thank you."

"Oh. By the way, I'm Sherri Hoving. Sherri. Sort of the grunt around here, do a little of everything, nothing of any real consequence."

This turned out to be so far from the truth—Sherri (short for Sherrifa, of all things) Hoving kept Ardent Publishing together with ingenuity, spit, and rubber bands, and, if not for her devotion and sapient governorship, this small concern would not stay afloat. It didn't take me long to learn this, and other necessary, hard-to-swallow truths.

I bided my time in their cramped waiting room, feeling as if I were being kept waiting only for show, but enjoying the view of Ms. Hoving's immaculate bare legs under her desk. Every few minutes—you could set your watch by it—she raised her freckled face toward me and smiled.

When I finally was ushered into Mr. Quillmeier's presence I found myself in an office not much larger than the waiting room, papers on every surface, the walls decorated with more book jacket blow-ups (*Mr. Anthony's Reproductive Organs, Flowers and Petals, The Scamp's Dog*) and along every wall stacks of books, about a hundred copies of each title.

Quillmeier was a piece of work himself. As round as a turnip with a mustache which appeared to be stuck on with sweat, he punched out a chubby-fingered hand and gave mine one quick pump.

"Sit down, Mr. Brackett," he said, gesturing toward the only other chair in the room, pushed uncomfortably close to the edge of his worn old desk.

"Thank you," I said, already formulating escape plans. This was certainly low-end publishing. How desperate was I to work in that rarefied atmosphere of disseminating literature to the great unwashed?

"Your resume," Quillmeier spurted.

I fumbled in my cardboard briefcase, which I tried to keep partially concealed between my knees. I pulled out a copy of my freshly printed resume and in so doing wrinkled it. I began an apology and a quick search for a second copy but Quillmeier snatched the proffered first copy from my sweating hand.

"Fine, fine," he said. He read it the way a child reads a history book. His concentration appeared to cause him pain as his face squinched, his left arm shot out involuntarily in spasm; he squirmed in his seat. It was an uncomfortable ten minutes before another word was spoken. I thought, flowers *and* petals?

"Starts at twenty a year," Quillmeier said, finally.

I hardly knew what to say. That was the interview?

"I hardly know what to say," I offered.

"Take it or leave it," Quillmeier said with a not-unfriendly, but somehow greasy smile.

"Can I sleep on it?" I asked, sheepishly.

"Nnn," he said, settling back into his well-broken-in chair. I thought I was almost dismissed. I thought to Mr. Quillmeier I was already a former applicant.

"No," I said. "No, I don't have to sleep on it. I'd be proud to work for Ardent," I said. I don't know where it came from.

"Fine, fine," Quillmeier said, rising ever so slightly from his seat and giving my hand one more fat pump. "Monday at nine, then?"

"Yes, surely," I said, backing out of his office.

In the anteroom Sherri Hoving was standing next to her desk, the whole, dark, willowy length of her, presented to view. She wore a smile that said *I knew you would get the job.*

A momentary queasiness overtook me. Sherri Hoving took a step toward me and put her arms around me, the way an aunt might hug a troubled nephew. I placed a tentative hand on the sweet, slick material over her lower back. Here was warmth, succor. Everything was going to be all right.

When I stepped out into the big city sunshine elation welled up inside me and I said to the lizard which lives inside us all, "I have a job in *publishing.*"

When I left Ardent it was still only 10:30 a.m. I first went to the bookstore and told Pat that I had found another job and would work out the remainder of the week if that was what he wanted. It was Thursday. It wasn't much notice. But Pat looked at me through his herbal haze and smiled a beatific smile and said, "Blessings on you, Brackett. Go out there and find the best damn authors you can. Make them write books that will shake the foundation of our constipated society. Draw from them their best work. Draw from them the words inside themselves that they are unaware of, words which lie dormant like an illness of rage. Publish, Brackett. Do good."

Well, I was somewhat taken aback. Part of me knew I wasn't exactly indispensable to The Book Inglenook, but I didn't expect such a divine sanction, such a heartfelt fare-thee-well.

"Well, damn, Pat," I said. "I will try to live up to your expectations. I will do my damnedest."

"I know you will, Brackett. Which publishing house has the good fortune to have picked up your worthy services, if I may ask?"

I hesitated. A foreboding came between us.

"Uh, a small concern. You might not know them. Little house called Ardent." I started to throw off a couple of their titles as if I had heard of them prior to my visit to their Lilliputian offices but Pat's expression was one of consternation, dismay, perhaps qualmishness.

"Ardent," he said like a book dropped on a dusty floor. He looked down at his desk in embarrassment.

"What's wrong?"

"Nothing. Nothing, Brackett. I thought, you know."

"I don't," I assured him.

"Well, it's just that they're a, a vanity house."

The words hit me in the solar plexus. The dreaded words hit me like being asked, "Can we just be friends?"

"Shit," I said.

"I'm sorry," Pat said. "Rain on the parade, that's me. Look, go there. Get started. Do the best you can and look for greener pastures. It won't be bad. It *is* publishing. Sort of."

I carried that "sort of" with me for the next couple of weeks. After leaving Pat (he said, go ahead, he really didn't need British Fiction re-alphabetized again) I treated myself to a real deli sandwich and an egg cream. I felt very New Yorkish, though that "sort of" sat in my stomach heavier than the sauerkraut on my Ruben. I called my parents that evening and told them I got a job in publishing and tried to make it sound lively, consequential, promising. I think it worked. My parents wouldn't know Alfred Knopf from Cima Academic & Language Media.

I wouldn't have thought it possible that they had room for me in the offices of Ardent Publishing, but when I went in that Monday morning, my cheap case stuck self-importantly under my armpit, they had cleared a corner of the anteroom (I can't imagine what was there before—I had no memory of a filing cabinet or couch or potted plant). There now was an old oak desk, the surface of which was as bare as a stone. Sherri Hoving gestured toward it like Vanna White toward a new SUV, and I returned her friendly smile. We were roommates.

"Wow," I said. "My own desk. It looks so pristine, so uninhabited. It appears ready to transact some majestic and transformative legerdemain. I hardly know how to become worthy of it."

"Well," Sherri said and bent her—have I already said willowy?—five-foot-nine-ish-frame over her own desk and fetched from it a stack of what I immediately recognized as manuscripts. There were a dozen or so of them. They were printed on various qualities of paper. Most were typewritten, if not composed on a word processor and printed in dot matrix or laser jet, but there were a couple copied in longhand on hundreds and hundreds of legal pad sheets, neatly stapled together. I sighed.

"Yep," Sherri Hoving said, relinquishing the burden to her new coworker, the sap. She practically washed her hands in Pilate's bowl.

I weighed them in my hands for comic effect, as if in so doing I could determine their value.

Sherri Hoving laughed. It was the sound of snowflakes falling on a harp. I was enchanted. I suddenly knew something new: Sherri Hoving enchanted me.

"Read them. Write up a page of synopsis and critique for the boss and then type a letter of acceptance to the author," she said, and was betrayed by a slight blush.

I wavered. "We accept them all?" I asked, though my pride was already an area of deep despoliation.

She opened a drawer in her desk and produced a fistful of checks.

"Fifteen checks. Fifteen manuscripts," she smiled, sheepishly. "We accept them all."

I sighed, set the stack on my desk, set myself down in the chair at my desk, which suddenly threatened to throw me around a bit, spinning like a dervish, its ancient spring so loose and disconnected. This bit of pratfall, perhaps, erased the tension of the moment.

Sherri tinkled again, again like the music of a harp, and I smiled a big, goofy grin.

"Welcome to the fast lane," she said and laughed again.

"I'm here to do my best," I said, a little too earnestly. And, then because that felt awkward I compounded the awkwardness. "Would you have dinner with me tonight?"

It was a complete surprise when to my unexpected question she barked out a quick *yes*, and was herself embarrassed by her enthusiasm.

So, my stint at Ardent Publishing began with mixed blessings. Sherri Hoving moved like a spring-borne fairy around that tiny room and every time she did my heart played the anvil chorus. And, meanwhile, I amused or depressed myself with the worst prose ever committed to paper. Ever, beginning with the Egyptians. It was mixed blessings all right.

That night I arrived at Sherri Hoving's apartment in one of the nicer buildings in the same area of uptown where Ardent was housed. She answered my buzz and when I found her on the third floor she was standing in the doorway to her apartment. She was wearing a sleeveless, short black dress, which set birds loose in me. Her long, bare legs were lightly tanned and sprayed gently with freckles, as were her delicious and pronounced shoulders. Her knees were brown biscuits. Her limbs were exquisite.

"Hello," she said, and I thought I detected a slight purr.

"Hello," I answered back. We moved into her rooms that were shockingly well-appointed. How much was she making at Ardent? Tasteful doesn't begin to describe how divinely laid out her apartment was. Interior decoration to me had always meant, "Where do I put the bookcase?" But, here, well, here was art.

"This is lovely," I said. And even though that sounded a tad fey my sincerity won the point.

"Thank you," she said.

We stood awkwardly near each other for a moment and I was about to ask for a restaurant recommendation when she stepped into my personal space and put her mouth against mine. The kiss—warm as life and moist enough to make its prolonged hold unbearably exciting—lasted until she turned her cheek slightly and exhaled as if she were overwhelmed.

"I've been wanting to do that since the first day you walked through the door at Ardent," she said.

"You haven't been alone," I said. It was almost right.

"Kiss me again," she said. I did.

That evening we spent on her plush, off-white couch, our tongues intertwined like the caduceus. And, while the making out (forgive the seventh-grade terminology) was erotic and moist and stimulating, it went no further. Oh, at one point, I believe, I cupped her small, bird-belly breast and she sighed and we kissed and kissed some more. I remember thinking, We have all the time in the world. We never did eat and I left around 2 a.m., my head spinning, my mouth refreshed as if I had drunk at Tantalus' pool, and my heart full of love, oh, overflowing love, for Sherrifa Hoving.

Over the ensuing months I was responsible for publishing numerous books under the Ardent imprint. My name appeared on them all as editor, though, in truth, my only addition to the stream which is literature was to make subjects and verbs agree (sometimes when they stubbornly seemed unwilling to, fighting like Kilkenny cats), clean up any language that strayed from the somewhat rocky path which is English grammar, take out the names of famous people in far-fetched tales of sexual misconducts (to stave off lawsuits, obviously) and substitute names of my own invention. This was at least creative and, at times, diverting. For instance, for John Kennedy I substituted Matt Chinoi, Snake Charmer. I replaced a particularly ugly reference to Calista Flockhart with the ridiculous name Sysipha Van Grubelhoffer. I turned Johnny Carson into Mungo Park. Etc. It was the only thing that made me feel as if I were not scooping up hot dung with my own well-trained hands and flinging it out the window onto the passersby below.

Some of the titles that left our offices with my name printed in garish Franklin Gothic on the copyright page were: *The Battle of the Bulge as Witnessed by Me and Tom Rasking* by Lt. Col. Gerald "Flip" Craig, *Senior Citizens Are Sexy, Too* by Jenny Vookles (that Jenny rankled, for a woman in her eighties), *Liposuction and You* by Dr. Vance Partridge, *Diddy-Wah-Diddy* by Resole McRey (surely a pseudonym—I wonder what *he* was hiding), *Tambourines, Pig-Whistles and Daisies in Gun Barrels: A Nomocanon of Poems* by Camel Jeremy Eros, *Huckleberry Finn, Racist* by Janet Grimace, *Love Gained, Lost, and Regained* by Anonymous (hmm), *Southern Jewism and the Delta: A Prototype* by Shlomo Einstein, *I Fought the Gulf War by My Own Damn Self* by Larry "Renegade" Yates, and on and on.

And, in truth, some of these dogs sold. I imagine what happens is the author's hometown bookstore, some mom-and-pop place called Book Land, or The Book Rack, orders a couple hundred for a signing, and the author's friends and family feel obliged to come and actually purchase a copy. At least our books are inexpensive, comparatively. But, of course, we can afford to be. We are totally subsidized up-front. And our author's contracts, well, I can't even discuss them. They are the special province of J. Quillmeier and J. Quillmeier alone. Who, by the way, is rarely in the office, the official statement being that he is having lunch with a client, or meeting with Japanese businessmen about overseas rights, or some such nonsense. But, those contracts, which are kept in locked files in his office, are as secret as the recipe for Coca-Cola. Very fishy, but I suspect our authors, for whom we promise to work very hard, pumping product out to the media-drenched society that awaits such drivel—we send out a single press release to a select group of bookstores and trade publications, total cost about $43—our poor deluded authors, I suspect, never have made a penny from their Ardent contracts. This is just supposition on my part, but it is not without some basis in evidence. But, that's another story and not this one, and, to be honest, what the hell do I care? These schnooks knew they were buying their way into authordom. What did they expect? Had they ever seen an Ardent title on the bestseller lists? Had an Ardent author ever been on Oprah? No, they knew the pond they were fishing in was stocked and the catch was a cheat, and they knew that in the end even the water in that pond would prove to be a sham, like the water under Casanova's boat in Fellini's film. I didn't care. Sorry.

The absence of the boss in the incommodious space of Ardent Publishing made for a sexual tension between Sherri and me, a delicious, daily sexual tension. Many days we spent with our respective tongues in each other's mouths, hands wandering the curvy landscapes that are the human body, heat rising like fervor from the devil's kitchen. But, beyond experiencing how lovely Ms. Hoving felt through her midsection, or where her hip gently swayed into her tender thighs, or circumnavigating the sweet meat of her upper arms, and down her choice lower back which effortlessly tipped into her incredible hindquarters, and all this mostly through whatever silken material covered her winsome body that day, nothing else happened between us. Every time the caloric vigor rose to danger levels—she could feel my need through the front of her brief skirts I am quite sure—we swayed away, we danced into a joking middle ground where there was only close friendship, companionship, *flirting*. It was frustrating, of course. About equally as frustrating as wading through those irksome manuscripts, feeling myself dipped in bad prose as if in machine oil, or a particularly adhesive oleo.

Meanwhile, Sherri was the most professional secretary/jackie-of-all-trades I'd ever witnessed or worked with. She literally did everything for Ardent, from mailing out the many letters of acceptance, to keeping the books (and cashing those mendacious checks), to acting as go-between between the elusive Mr. Quillmeier and *anyone* else. I composed my own letters of acceptance (oh, sorry, lies! oh, loathsome soft-soap!) and for that, and for my two-hundred--word synopses, I called myself an editor. I collected a paycheck that allowed me to live in the hub of the publishing industry, the city that never sleeps.

It was around my one-year anniversary at Ardent (my parents in their frequent phone calls and letters were fond of repeating to me the gloating and inflated remarks they made to their septuagenarian friends about their big-shot son), after a particularly dispiriting evening at Sherri's (we had actually unzipped a couple of pieces of clothing, almost touching various body parts through only one sheer layer of undergarment), I arrived about thirty minutes late to the office.

"Hey, hotshot," Sherri said, a shy, almost-frightened smile tempting the corners of her syrupy mouth.

"Hey, Sherri," I dropped.

"You okay? You look a little bedraggled. Maybe bed-raggled, eh?"

This was sexy banter to her, I suddenly realized. She thought what we had done the previous evening was highly erotic, would garner a couple of Xs at least. Were there really young women this innocent living in New York City? The notion seemed ludicrous and I admit I was a bit cross.

"Not raggled enough, perhaps, lover?" I practically snarled.

Her face retreated like a beaten cur. She turned to her desk and made a show of shuffling the papers. She turned with a snap and held out a slim stack of telltale, ecru 8 ½ x 11 envelopes.

I groaned.

"Mail's here already," she said, throwing a slight lilt into her speech, a pitiful attempt to cajole me into our old style.

"Thanks," I said and took the stack as if it were a flattened and exenterated piece of road kill.

I sat at my desk and stared at the return addresses for many minutes, stalling, trying to gather what wits I had left. The work came from all over. America was awash in wannabe writers. There was Abe Peters, Lincoln, Nebraska; Rory Canseco, Wind River, Wyoming; Lauralyn "Laurie" Enos,

Fidelity, Georgia; Lamar Negri, Page, Washington (a writer's town, surely!); Kenny the Snake Girardi, Somerville, Tennessee. It was all so—debilitating. I was tired just holding these monstrosities. I punched them aside, dismissively. I couldn't do it. Not that day. Maybe never again.

I don't know what caught my attention, what about the envelope made it stick out—maybe it simply *stuck out*, lay uncovered in the cast-aside heap. The envelope itself was smudged, as if handled by a car mechanic. Were it evidence in a police investigation the culprit's prints were readable with a naked eye—there was no need to send these babies to the lab in Washington. And the return address said, simply, "City." Presumably, this meant this labor of love came from somewhere within the confines of our sprawling megalopolis. It was addressed "Ardent Publishing. Fiction Editor." And our address. Written in blurry pencil, as if from inside an aquarium. It was a wonder it made it to us, so indecipherable was the penmanship, so childlike the scrabble.

It was an exotic enough piece of communication that I slit it open right away. The yellow ledger-pad paper tumbled out as if enchanted, as if the pieces of foolscap were fey genii released from their bottle. They made a mad pile on my desk, papers from hell, or some suburb of hell reserved for the work of the crazed, for the products of contaminated minds. They scared me somehow, covered as they were with that same penciled scrawl, which seemed alive on the page, like some particularly loathsome form of insectivore, one which found its way into your bedclothes at night, one which entered your body through the soles of your feet and lodged someplace vital and vulnerable, slowly poisoning you, slowly fusing or liquefying your entire inner self. They were chthonic.

Yet, I could not look away.

The top sheet bore what I imagined was the title, flung across the head, above where the lines began, like on a school report. And the title was *Anima*, certainly a broad-enough topic, I thought. And in more crabbed alphabetiforms, as if it pained the poor soul to pin his name on the page, as if, indeed, by pinning it there he may have trapped himself, below the larger title, it said: by Jim Nozoufist. And, of course, there amid the detritus which was his book lay his check, which I barely registered except to notice it was at least made out in ballpoint to Ardent Publishing, Publisher.

Ridiculous, I thought. Ridiculous title, absurd nom de plume. Who was this wise guy kidding? And, somewhere in the middle of my nonsensical fear, a small anger grew, a misplaced anger at this ridiculous Jim Nozoufist and his unsanitary manuscript. How dare he, I huffed. I sat back hard in my chair, which once again tilted dangerously, like a rolling log over a chasm. Sherri looked around hopefully with a can-I-help look on her exquisite, colorful face. I scowled back.

After a moment I picked up page one of *Anima* and began to read. I read the first sentence with a self-righteous mad on. I read the second sentence with a prickle-like fever at the back of my neck. I read the third sentence, a sculpted piece of prose mastery worthy only of some pixilated offspring of Beckett and Virginia Woolf, with a growing sense of disbelief. Oh, my lares and penates!

An hour passed. Two. Somewhere beyond the periphery of my mindfulness I was cognizant of a sulking Sherri who went about her work, left for lunch, returned. It was four o'clock in the afternoon when I threw down the pages I still had in my hand and craned my stiff neck heavenward. It was unbelievable. It was preposterous. I looked guiltily around me, as if I had smuggled some plutonium and was squirreling it away in my desk drawer, or as if I had just inherited the secrets of eternal life and did not want to share them with anyone. Not even my sweetheart, not even my parents. Sherri turned inquisitively toward me but my face must have seemed deranged, goggle-eyed, for she crinkled her nose and widened her beautiful mahogany blinkers and turned back to her own work. I took a series of deep breaths and leaned back precipitously in my chair. What was first an inkling of something *other* had become a faith in something grand. I had on my desk a masterpiece. A piece of the puzzle, the missing pieces perhaps in the puzzle of world literature. Or, so I felt initially.

No. It was stronger than that. I was sure. This was *it*. This was *the real thing*. And I was an editor at a dog assed, corrupt publishing concern that would take this precious cargo and jettison it upon the world like another book of grandma's poetry, like another memoir of "My Most Memorable Character." I surged with power, but it was a power checked, a light under a bushel, a light obliterated and trapped under a sleazy, perplexing bushel. But my metaphors run away. I had to think. I had to clear my mind and figure out *what to do*.

I gathered the pages and stuffed them back into their envelope (they didn't want to fit, as if once oxygen had reached them they had expanded, full of life, or as if they would not be imprisoned again, ever again). I made a quick, rude excuse to Sherri, rushed past her, and went immediately home.

I must keep *Anima* with me at all times. I must never let it out of my sight. These were my thoughts.

And I must find Jim Nozoufist. And tell him—what? That he was a genius, that he had written the most important novel since Joyce reconfigured things. Needless to say, I reread the book in its entirety that night—it took me until the wee hours—and it only reinforced my opinion. This was the book that the literary world had been waiting for. It was an answer to questions we didn't even dare ask, questions we didn't know needed asking. And I owned it. *Anima* was mine.

2

The address listed for the author of *Anima* was in a tony part of Manhattan, a part, quite honestly, where I rarely ventured, where the word penthouse was tossed around lightly, where the recirculated air was ripe with the scent of freshly minted cash. Was it possible this adept was worth more than the entire publishing concern on which he was pinning his literary aspirations? Why didn't the joker just publish the book himself, certainly a time-honored way of appearing in print, and just slightly more expensive than turning over blood money to Ardent?

After some initial wrangling with a taciturn doorman, who insisted there was no one living in Two Towers by the name of Jim Nozoufist, a call was made to the apartment number written as the return address on the soiled envelope I had clenched under my jacket. (I had spent the earliest hours of the morning at Kinko's making a copy of *Anima*, which now resided in the locked drawer of my desk in my apartment.) Some muted conversation was made into the phone, while I stood by like a miscreant pupil, some description given of the personage wishing admittance I imagined, and after hanging up the doorman simply opened the inner door without apology or even assent. I walked past him, hiking up my dignity, looking into his dead eyes as I walked unnecessarily close to him and into Two Towers.

The elevator stopped on the thirteenth floor and I bobbed down the thickly carpeted corridor to Apartment 1307 and lightly rapped on the door. After a few sweaty moments—was there another gauntlet to run before admittance?—the door opened and an astoundingly beautiful woman in her mid-to-late fifties stood there glittering like a prize. Her jewelry glittered, her dress glittered, her teeth glittered, even her décolletage, sprinkled with some kind of glitter makeup, glittered. She was smiling to beat the band.

"Mr. Brackett?" she twinkled.

"Yes," I said, transfixed by her. "Call me Todd." I was so nervous it came out "Dodd."

"Please come in."

I walked in as if I was being led past the Pearly Gates, mesmerized as much by this ideal of womanhood as by the incredible space into which I was coaxed. It might have been Gloria Vanderbilt's home, or, indeed, one of the nicer salas in heaven. If my conscious brain was working at all it was chewing on the question, who is this ravishing dowager and what does she have to do with J. Nozoufist?

"Please sit," she gestured toward the plushest piece of furniture I had ever seen. I could have lived in it.

A gentleman appeared as if a bell sash had been pulled.

"Would you like some refreshment?" this lovely woman asked, all flickering eyes and teeth.

"No. Uh, actually, yes, some ice tea, if available," I managed.

"Ice tea, Noah," she spoke to the superannuated butler, and I assumed he really was the Biblical patriarch.

"I'm sorry, Mr. Brackett. How rude of me. I am Cecilia Quisby. My name may be familiar to you, though I'm well aware that it is not me who you are here to see."

I didn't know her from Betty Grable but I smiled and nodded. She seemed to know a lot more about whatever was happening than I did and in such situations I always find it best to keep mum until things begin to take shape. It didn't take long.

"You are looking for Jim," Cecilia Quisby shimmered.

"Yes," I said. "I'm from Ardent Pub—"

"Yes, I know. Jim sent you his book. I told him we could look elsewhere, but, well, Jim has a sort of stubbornness to him, which…"

She drifted away momentarily and I took the opportunity to try and win some respect from this imposing woman.

"Frankly, Mrs. Quisby—"

"Cecilia."

"Cecilia. Frankly, I think, just maybe, Mr. Nozoufist has written something really remarkable here."

"No," Cecilia Quisby spoke quickly and then caught herself. "I mean, really? It's, it's good?'

"Um, yes. I believe it is quite good."

"Well, I'll be damned. Excuse my Alabama-backyard French," she said and sort of fell back into the couch, wherein she could have fallen quite a long way.

"Jim is a real writer, then?"

"I believe so."

"Hm," she said and she lay there, in a repose rather unladylike for someone so elegant, though it gave me ample time to run my eyes over her aged but stately figure. She was a supernatural being.

"Mrs. Quisby—Cecilia—who is Jim Nozoufist? Is he here? I would really love the opportunity to speak with him about his book and about the possibilities I think—"

"Jim's not here at the moment, Todd," she spoke, familiarly, and she rose to a more upright posture and placed a warm hand on my knee. It burned through my cheap suit pants. Up my leg went the heat of torment.

Letting the fluster pass, I took a difficult swallow of ice tea, which Noah had delivered I know not when, but which, magically, appeared near my right hand.

"Is Jim Nozoufist your husband, ma'am?" I don't know where the Southernism came from, triggered possibly by her mention of Alabama.

She let loose a cachinnate fanfare. "Oh, my, no," she said. "Jim, well, Jim works for me."

"As?" I asked without thought.

"Oh, odd jobs. When a woman reaches my age she needs some seeing to. Jim does a little driving for me, a little grocery shopping, that sort of thing."

"I see. Well, I don't want to take up too much of your time. When can I speak to him? It's rather urgent," I added, self-importantly.

"Noah," Cecilia Quisby spoke in conversational tones and the man was suddenly there. "Call Jim and have him come straight over."

Noah nodded, I think, and left the room.

Cecilia smiled her bright white smile at me and we sat in silence for a few moments and I sipped the ice tea without tasting it.

After a while she scooted a half-inch closer to me, leaned forward, and replaced the hand on my knee, perhaps a measurable space higher on my thigh. This woman knew men. She knew me and she had me and she knew she had me. I didn't care. It was literature a-calling and, for the moment, even the sexual flirtation of such an attractive woman took a backseat.

"Todd," she said, as if about to let me in on a family secret. "Prepare yourself for Jim. He may not be what you were expecting."

"Okay," I said, though I wasn't aware of expecting anything.

A moment later there was the sound of activity coming from the kitchen area.

"I believe he's here now," Cecilia Quisby said, rising from the couch. Putting space between us was both a relief and an agony.

What emerged from the rear of the apartment was indeed not what I had expected no matter what I had expected. Neanderthal was an unavoidable reference term and had I Tourrette's syndrome no doubt I would have spoken the word aloud. Jim Nozoufist was a man about the same age as Mrs. Quisby, though through grime and facial hair it was difficult to ascertain much about him. He was positively pithecoid. Surely this was just some poor homeless gull they brought up to impersonate the author. His dungy attire— ankle-length, soot-gray raincoat, unbuttoned formerly white shirt, oversize achromatic pants, squalid, unlaced high-tops— reminded me of the costume Ian Anderson of Jethro Tull used to sport in his early rhythm-and-blues days, a sort of crazed, exhibitionist, street person affectation. Indeed he somewhat resembled Mr. Anderson in the uncouthness of his wild appearance. Aqualung with an Olivetti, I thought. No one could have been more out of place in Cecilia Quisby's elegant apartment.

"Jim, come here," Cecilia beckoned with a bejeweled hand. "This is Todd Brackett from Ardent Publishing. He's here about your book."

No change of expression occurred on the exanimate face of the feral fellow. Did he understand? Was he capable of more than animal instinct?

He shuffled forward and extended a meaty and distinctly unclean hand. I took it gently but he squeezed like an Irishman in a pub contest and when I drew my smarting body part back I found myself imagining all sorts of disease, scrud or double scrud. I wanted to bolt for the bathroom.

Professionalism reigned.

"Mr. Nozoufist? As Mrs. Quisby said, I'm from Ardent and I've had the pleasure of reading your manuscript, your, um, novel, *Anima*, and I'm quite taken with it. I believe you have a real gift. I have taken it upon myself to contact you personally, not standard procedure perhaps at Ardent, but I was moved to do so by the particularity of your work, by its special otherness, which it is my belief may just be something very special in the world of contemporary letters." I felt as if I was talking to an actor standing in for the real author. At no time during my speech did I believe this was the author of the book I still had clenched inside my jacket. I also felt orotund and absurd in my language and as if I was talking over the poor man's head.

There now emerged from somewhere beneath the whiskers and grime on Mr. Nozoufist's facade a deep growl or grumble. Bubbles of saliva formed in his mustache. Fear flashed through me—perhaps he was an epileptic, perhaps he was about to bite my neck—but I glanced at Cecilia and she was smiling beatifically. This calmed me somewhat.

"I'd like Ardent to publish *Anima*," he said.

I nodded and was about to open negotiations—whatever those were going to be—when he sputtered further.

"Cecilia sent the check. We've paid," he said, and looked to his patron for reassurance. Cecilia moved to him and took his filthy arm in hers and placed a kiss on his hispid cheek. He smiled, a horrible smile, a monster's lascivious grin.

It suddenly occurred to me that Jim Nozoufist did a little more than some grocery shopping for this woman. There was a warmth between them one sees in movies, that romantic shorthand that says, *intimacy*. It made me feel unwell for some reason.

"Mr. Nozoufist, rest assured that all is satisfactory in your prepayment and the contract that denotes. Ardent would be proud to publish your novel. Ardent would be more than proud. Ardent should get down on its collective knees (here a brief flash of Sherri's lovely face threw a blinding flare over my vision) and beg to publish *Anima*. What I'm saying is—"

And, here I was at the moment of truth, the moment I had been dreading. What was my plan? Did I think I could parlay this man's talent, this wild man's exotic talent, into some kind of score for Todd Brackett? What were my motives? I had convinced myself that they were pure and that the main thing, the *important* thing, was to get this book into print and into wide distribution, where it could, rightly or wrongly, upset the placid and smug and dull ship of state that was modern fiction.

"What is it, Todd?" Cecilia asked with genuine concern in her voice.

"I think *Anima* may be the greatest novel of its, of our, time."

I said it. I laid it out there like a taunt and I did not know, in this extraordinary company, where such a taunt would lead. I did not know who would pick it up.

After a pregnant moment, our aberrant author spoke.

"You do work for Ardent, don't you?" It was somewhere between a growl and a barroom challenge.

"Yes, yes," I assured. "But, this book, this marvelous book, is something quite uncommon. Quite frankly, it is too good for Ardent. I mean, we are fine for what we do, but, Mr. Nozoufist, Jim, if I may, *Anima* needs one of the big boys. It needs a Knopf, a Farrar Straus & Giroux. It needs a Gary Fisketjohn. It needs a Liz Darahnsof. It needs paperback rights, foreign rights, electronic rights, Hollywood representation, for Christ's sake!" I was sweating. "This is a major book. A searingly significant, important book." I finished with a deep breath as if I had sprinted here from Newark.

"I don't understand a word you're saying," Cecilia Quisby let out. "And I'm sure Jim doesn't either. With your Fiskyjons and your Jews and your Darryn Soft, Mr. Brackett, Todd, we are simple people. What are you suggesting?"

I didn't know. Could I tell them I didn't know? That even I was out of my depth?

"I don't know," I said.

"Ardent's good enough for me," the musty giant now spat out and strode from the room so quickly it left me speechless. I looked at Cecilia Quisby—she smiled like the opening of the moon—and a few minutes later I was walking back toward Ardent, shell-shocked. The manuscript was still tucked under my jacket and my arm was cramped from the tension of holding it there. I had never even brought it out, examined it in front of its exotic creator, showed him that I knew my way around a work of fiction. I only then understood that it was what I had desired—to prove myself to the author of such an eccentric masterpiece. I had expected to be parlaying with someone along the lines of Mervyn Peake or Alexander Theroux.

Cecilia Quisby was right. I hadn't expected Jim Nozoufist. I hadn't expected a madman. And, now, where were we?

Sherri was playing coy when I returned to the office, playing at avoiding my eyes but giving me uncertain, saucy side-glances at every opportunity. I sat at my desk and stared straight ahead. My head was full of expensive perfume and deodorized penthouse air and Cecilia Quisby's squeezable bosom and her hand, which generated heat like a magnifying glass, and the sweet rot of old flesh and fetid clothing and the incredible, exploding encyclopedia, which hovered above it all, that book called *Anima*. I finally remembered to unclench my arm and release the manuscript and I laid it in front of me, atop the numerous unopened envelopes that would make up Ardent's spring list.

I believe Sherri hissed or made some noise, which was not quite human speech, and I slowly turned toward her. She smiled a delicate, infirm smile.

My heart beat hard once or twice—there was pain there—should I worry? And then I opened my arms and Sherri Hoving slid across the room and onto my lap and her warm mouth covered mine and her tongue swelled into me and I lost, momentarily, all my worries as my blood careened in my body looking for the place it was needed most. It found my loins.

Sherri felt the stiffening there and she loosened her kiss slightly and looked into my eyes. Her hand went south, where the trouble was, and opened my tensions to the air and it was that hand job at my desk—that release—in the middle of a most troublesome workday, which began to crystallize things for me. Which began to set a course for myself, for Sherri Hoving, and for our demented ward, the foul and priestly Jim Nozoufist.

Through Cecilia Quisby I set up a meeting with our author for the following day at a coffee shop near Ardent and I asked Sherri to join us. My reasons for doing this were a bit confused, but it's safe to say I wanted a witness. I wanted backup. And I counted on her to be true to her pseudo-lover and I counted on her unique capacity for organization, something this situation was in desperate need of.

I sketched the situation for Sherri and throughout my extravagant tale she looked at me wide-eyed, her moist mouth forming a series of variations on ohs and ovals. At the end of my recitation—and I told her almost everything, including my reticence about seeing this work of literature go through the mill which was vanity publishing—her doe eyes blinked once or twice and then she was all business. I told you she was the glue that held Ardent together and that professionalism took over and she immediately began making notes and gathering together a file, a file that would remain a secret between her and me, under the name "Anima, Nozoufist." The Anima, Nozoufist file. I believe she felt that this secret was further cement to our "understanding," though, for the time being, the personal was a back burner for me.

We arrived at the coffee shop about fifteen minutes early, such was our excitement and nervousness to set this thing into motion, whatever this thing was to be. With Sherri's encouragement our plan was simple, at least as far as Step One went. Beyond Step One was a haze of possibility, a scrim over the future which seemed murky and confusing and even perhaps a little dangerous, though I didn't at the time have anything to be afraid of. We sat over our dry bagels and weak joe and our conversation was scant and clipped, airy like a tattered flag. The fifteen minutes passed and then another fifteen and Sherri looked at me with an anxiety in her boyishly resplendent features which was overflowing with sympathy and concern. I believe she might have, for just a moment, believed I had made up Jim Nozoufist out of whole cloth, however exotic that cloth would have to be. I admit that I even had the passing notion that I had imagined the man, something from some primitive consciousness welling up like a bad dream, something unreal, a bit of undigested beef perhaps.

Just as exasperation began to take over I saw through the shop's wide glass window the madman author striding our way, crossing against traffic as if he were indestructible, walking almost totally erect. To say he burst into the coffee shop is to resort to cliché, but Nozoufist practically thrust the door off its hinges, so exaggeratedly violent was his ingress. Sherri jumped in her seat as I stood to beckon the Yeti over. Jim wore the same outfit I had seen him in earlier. Sherri wore a look of what might be described as professional doubt, mixed with, I think, bemusement.

The waitress eyed us askance now but took our order for another cup of their dishwater coffee and a round of eggs and toast for our guest.

"Jim," I began, "This is Sherri Hoving from our office."

"Pleased," Jim grunted and put a hoary hand out, which missed Sherri's delicate attempt at a handshake and ended up gripping her forearm as if this were a meeting of two Vikings.

Step One was this: we were going to convince Jim Nozoufist to make us his independent agents. Sherri had sketched out a contract that gave us full power to place *Anima* where we thought best and make what demands we could, reaping only a measly 15 percent of whatever profits befell us. The important thing, the *only* thing, was to get *Anima* into bookstores, onto library shelves, into the right critics' hands, to get the damn thing *recognized*. The inchoate contract also gave full editorial decision making to Todd Brackett, but with final say on any changes to the author.

Nozoufist seemed to chew on these terms at about the same frenetic and unwholesome way he dug into his toast and eggs. We could not look at him and spent those tense minutes looking at each other with, for want of a better word, affection. Our eyes may have been dewy.

"Ardent doesn't want it," he said, finally.

"No, no," I quickly corrected him. "Ardent would publish it in a heartbeat. Cash Cecilia's check and throw *Anima* out there. But, you have to understand Ardent would publish the ravings of any lunatic who could muster the money to pay their fees. They would publish that surly waitress's love poems to her trucker boyfriend. Ardent is not about editorship. Ardent is about taking money from people who are desperate to have something, anything, in print. *Anima* on the other hand is a life-changing work of the imagination. We can take it just about anywhere we want and get some real attention generated. We can make you famous, if that's not putting an inappropriate slant on it."

"Ardent is for the odes or autobiographies of retired doctors and lawyers who have nothing better to do with the money they've made grinding the noses of the poor," Sherri put in. I squeezed her knee.

"Hmm," Jim Nozoufist said, maybe through his nose.

"We'll take full responsibility," I added. "If we fail to produce anything greater—but there is little chance of that—we can always fall back on Ardent."

"Okay, then," the mammalian author said, rising quickly from his seat. This time his handshakes hit their marks and he was gone, seemingly carried out by a gust of wind from the reek of New York, a wind up from the subways, smelling of urine and lost dreams and the foul decay of a once-great city.

Sherri and I looked at each other. She couldn't suppress a tight giggle.

"Well, we got what we wanted," she said. "What next?"

"I'll make some calls," I said. "You make up a formal contract and we'll get it to Mr. Nozoufist and get this ball rolling." I smiled with a confidence that was the confidence of a child becoming an adult. I was making it.

Sherri and I walked back into the office holding hands like Hansel and Gretel, cooing at each other, snickering like schoolchildren. We were met by the grim countenance of our plenitudinous boss.

"Hello, Mr. Quillmeier, "Sherri said, seriously suddenly, with more aplomb than I could have mustered.

"Early lunch?" he asked.

"Meeting with an author," I said, but from Sherri's darting eyes I knew I had blundered.

"We don't meet with authors," J. Quillmeier firmly informed me. "We publish their shitty books and cash their checks and move on."

"Is that on our logo?" I asked, sarcasm borne of this newly acquired and foolhardy confidence.

Mr. Quillmeier glowered. He placed a chubby hand on a chubby hip and looked us over as if he didn't quite know what we were up to, into mother's cosmetics, perhaps, or sneaking out back with the airplane glue.

"Who is this author who demands such attention?" he asked.

It was a fair question. Unfortunately, it caught the two of us answerless. We stared straight ahead. My armpits filled with moisture.

J. Quillmeier had us and let us run, cruelly, like hooked fish, which he only wanted the barb to dig deeper into. He stood before us like the Colossus of Rhodes for a few minutes while we fidgeted and cleared our throats.

"Was it perhaps James Nozoufist?" he asked.

We were stricken. We looked stricken.

"How—" was as far as I got.

"Cecilia Quisby is a very old and dear friend, my compatriots. She phoned me at home to find out how long until we could expect to see her man's book in the bookstores."

"Cecilia Quisby told me she tried to talk Nozoufist out of publishing with Ardent," I said, floundering, fighting for my life.

"A blind. She sent the book in through the regular channels, but, still was not above a phone call to an old admirer to grease the works. Seems she had a visit, a peculiar visit, from our chief editor who did nothing but confuse her about our intentions. Quite inappropriate. Hence, the call."

"Ahem," I believe I said.

J. Quillmeier waited.

"Mr. Quillmeier, this book, by this friend of your friend, is, well, it's quite a book."

"And?"

"And I think, maybe, it's just, sort of, not for Ardent."

J. Quillmeier waited another painful heartbeat, looked at me, looked with not a little disappointment at Sherri, and then spoke, with decisive finality.

"You're fired," he said, poking a sausage-shaped finger at my sternum.

"And you," he said, hesitating as he turned toward the soul of his publishing house, and in that moment of hesitation, Sherri Hoving, God bless her, moved in my direction and slipped her frabjous arm through mine in a show of confederacy. "Well, you're fired, too," he was forced to add.

He then rolled into the inner recesses of his private den, a bear that must certainly go into hibernation, at least temporarily, with no Sherri Hoving around to keep his affairs in order.

"Well," I said, exhaling for the first time in ten minutes.

"We're out on the street," Sherri said, with brave calm.

"But we have *Anima*," I said. And I think I really believed it was a charm, a shield, a mojo against the perilous future.

Of course, in the following days, there was a back-and-forth wrangle between myself and J. Quillmeier about who indeed did own the rights to the wondrous Gordian knot which was *Anima*. It was the most conversation I had with the man in the nearly thirteen months since I had come to work for him. He was a surprisingly savvy combatant. I say surprisingly, because, one must ask, what is he doing running this shill game for suckers if he has the smarts to do better work.

It was my, our, contention that the author had signed a binding contract with us (he actually had not at this time, but the contract was professionally drawn up by my amorous conspirator and awaited only a meeting with the author for the proverbial eyes to be crossed, etc.) and that he had no such contract with Ardent Publishing. It was J. Quillmeier's retort, as one might expect, that the check, which he had quickly cashed, from Cecilia Quisby, constituted a contract and one which he had already made moves to justify by putting the manuscript through the motions of getting into shoddy print and between two glued-together cardboard covers and hence turned into a proud Ardent book. I doubted this contention, simply because we had both copies of the manuscript, and though it was possible he had obtained another from Cecilia Quisby, J. Quillmeier had neither the means nor the wherewithal to get the whole process rolling by his own rolling self. At least, this is what Sherri and I fervently hoped.

We believed, though, that we had to move quickly.

We set up another meeting with Jim in the coffee shop (as we now began to call him whenever we referred to him, the familiarity meaning—what?—a confidence that he was ours, that we were going to ride his raggle-taggle coattails into literary stardom). We anticipated trouble arranging said meeting, but Cecilia betrayed no loyalty to her old friend JQ, and readily set us up with our author but she also did not offer *his* address. It was an unspoken part of the dealings that everything would be funneled through the glamorous and ladylike hands of Cecilia Quisby.

Jim was late again. Sherri and I sat in worried silence, holding hands lightly, fingertips to fingertips, across the tabletop, casting strained, grim smiles at each other as each additional five minutes ticked away. Finally, Jim was blown in, by that same ill wind, leaves and detritus seemingly swirling around him, his hair a tangled mass, full of birds' nests and insect larvae and perhaps the missing body of James Hoffa. He threw himself into the booth on Sherri's side, fairly slamming against her but not upending her tight smile.

"Okay," he began, as if he had called this meeting. He was all at once in charge and it momentarily upset me.

"What you got for Old Jim?" he asked, a piratical jolliness inflecting his voice, unlike anything we had heretofore witnessed.

"A contract," Sherri said, briskly, whipping it out from her briefcase and laying it on the yolk-stained Formica.

Jim looked down at it the way first man must have looked at first fire.

"It says, basically, what?" Jim said, quickly, as if to hide his embarrassment at not understanding the legal jargon before him. "You own me. You own *Animus*. You get all the money."

I didn't know if he was kidding or not. I didn't know if he was capable of kidding.

"Of course not," I said. "Just as we discussed. We will do everything in our power, *everything* to see that *Animus* gets the publishing contract it deserves, including all foreign rights, paperback rights, etc. at the best house possible and for the most money available. We vow to do this not only on this piece of paper in front of you but, here, to your face, with honest and heartfelt integrity. We will get your book the attention it deserves and for that we get 15 percent of all profits."

"15 percent," Jim said.

"That's fairly common, low even. Understand, Mr. Nozoufist, we have given up all other work to pursue this. We have no other job but getting this book out and reaping the rewards it deserves. We have, you might say, put all our eggs in one basket, laid our whole lives on the line," Sherri put in.

Nozoufist looked at me with what I thought was a twinkle in his eye—he resembled briefly a deranged Santa Claus—and then at Sherri the same way. Suddenly he leant over and kissed my compatriot full on the mouth, pulling back like a drunkard who has just taken a large draught of a rich ichor. A smile opened up the box of snakes which was his visage.

"Let's do it," he said.

I was taken aback. But then I smiled just as quickly and took his callused hand into mine and gave it a hearty shake. Fellow-feeling flowed.

Sherri, recovering from her bestial buss, pointed a red-nailed finger at the line on the contract where Jim was to put his John Hancock and brought out a pen from her lap with which he would sign. Jim gripped the pen like it was a Louisville Slugger. Just for a second I thought he might make a crude *X* on the space provided, but he signed with a flourish, his name a dance of curlicues and embellishment, ending with a singular paraph.

"Good," he said. And he was gone.

Although tangential to the tale, now might be the time to discuss the nature of the relationship so recently born between the lithe Sherri Hoving and your humble narrator. After that unexpected office manipulation of my *membrum virile*, I supposed, naturally, that we had embarked on that journey that takes a couple of ordinary human beings and transforms them into the *coniunctio spirituum;* in short, that we were now a fully feathered couple, free to partake of each other's intimacies, privileged to feel the human warmth and moisture at the heart of the creature called man (and woman). I thought, bluntly put, that we would be fucking, and soon.

It was not to be. Instead we regressed. That workaday pizzle-pull was not repeated and when our tongue-sucking grew too intense Sherri again began that coy retreat that had initially signaled to me that we were not to be, couple-wise. It was frustrating and may or may not bear on the frustrations to follow. I am not a Freudian disciple and do not pretend to possess the ability to explain human endeavor in terms of inner chemistry, misfiring neurons, bad potty training, want of breastfeeding as a child. So what follows followed. My flesh-loneliness is, most probably, only a not-so-interesting sidebar.

The truth was we couldn't place *Anima*. Much to my chagrin and shock, even when we were able to get the thing into what I would have supposed to be sympathetic hands, we got kind dismissals, compliments galore, but no takers. Roger Giroux himself penned a quick note, calling the book a "spiritual cousin to *Confederacy of Dunces*," but his house passed on it, seemingly against his wishes, but it's hard to tell. And, besides, I thought, Jim Nozoufist could write rings around that poor dead Louisianian. If he were alive, I guess I mean.

I was flummoxed. I was confounded and astonished. We tried half a dozen major houses, both Sherri and I calling in whatever tenuous connections we boasted, and received little or no encouragement. Could it be that I was wrong about *Anima*, about its place in the line of literature which went from Homer to Rabelais to Sterne to Joyce and then, unerringly, I believed, to our own beloved dement. No, I was not wrong. This was a hell of a book, a world-beater. It was the times that were to blame. I was not the first to decry the shallowness that had overtaken the culture, from idiotic TV, to bright, shiny, big-spectacle movies as empty as raided graves, to art which only imitated art which had self-consciously imitated art before it but at least for a laugh, right up to and including the now conglomerate-controlled publishing houses, where there were only *acquisitions* editors, where there was the search for the next *Bridges of Madison County* ongoing, but not the next Thomas Pynchon. I knew it. I knew it all. Maxwell Perkins was dead, as dead as Marley. I knew it but I still hoped. Surely, there was a place for genius still, a place for something as fresh and new and invigorating as Jim Nozoufist and his cracked, portmanteau tome.

Six months passed in this way. Increasingly frantic phone calls, faxes, letters, cold-call visits to houses we only knew the names of. We worked out of Sherri's apartment, where it was comfortable and clean and she cooked wonderful meals of couscous and exotic vegetables. She told me to stop worrying about money and I did, for minutes at a time, but things were not going well. Soon we would have to admit that we had to look for work—continue our ceaseless search for a home for *Anima*—but, at the same time, do something, however menial, to pay the bills.

It was about this time when I got a call from Cecilia Quisby. She was concise on the phone, but not unfriendly, and she wanted the four of us to get together to discuss the future of Jim's book. I was to pick her up at half-past seven and proceed to her private club, where a dinner would be waiting for us, over which we could make some plans on what to do next. It sounded good. It sounded wrong. But, what choice did we have?

Also, she added, could Ms. Hoving pick Jim up, and she rattled off a quick address.

I arrived at Two Towers at seven-fifteen, dressed in my best suit, which was a poor imitation of good grooming, nervous as sunlight. This time the doorman parted the waters for me immediately and I proceeded up to Cecilia Quisby's wondrous place of residence, feeling like a kid on a first date.

Knowing my early arrival was rude I rapped lightly on Cecilia's door. It took some ninety seconds or so—an eternity—before the door was opened and there stood Dame Quisby herself. I had, of course, expected Lurch and was embarrassed to find Cecilia at the door dressed only in a housecoat, albeit a sheer, sparkling housecoat. The shins which showed beneath the elegant hem of her garment, though aged, shone like ambergris and her toenails were painted a pale shade of lavender, which made my heart do a sad drumroll.

"I'm so sorry I'm early," I sputtered.

"Nonsense," she said, waving me in.

I shuffled in, a child, a nullity in her reflective radiance.

"I'm afraid Noah is off for the evening, so if you could just make yourself comfortable while I dress," she said gesturing vaguely toward all that was hers.

"Certainly," I said.

She wafted away toward her bedroom and I spent some time examining the art on the walls. All the names were familiar. All the paintings were authentic.

"We're not having much luck with Jim's book," she called from the recesses of her apartment. It was a statement, almost, but not quite, a challenge.

"No," I admitted. I began my rant about the unappreciated prophet, the overemphasized profit, etc. She cut me off with a reverberating contralto.

"La di da, Todd," she sang. "You underestimate yourself. You have literature in your veins."

I let a few moments pass. I had no answer.

"Is that not true?" she asked, this time the challenge more clearly delineated.

"Well, I've tried all I know. I've called in all my markers. I've—"

"Todd. Todd, come here," she spoke, as if I were her stubborn spaniel.

I walked slowly toward the doorway to her bedroom. I didn't want to go there. I was sore afraid.

I stood in the doorway but my eyes were on my shoes.

"Look at me, Todd," she commanded.

I raised my face, knowing what would be there. Cecilia Quisby sat on the edge of her bed putting her stockings on. They were the kind that stayed up only by the magic of their darker top halves. I was looking at quite a bit of the fifty-year-old Cecilia Quisby and I was thoroughly impressed by what

NOTES TOWARD THE STORY AND OTHER STORIES

she was showing me. Her body, covered here and there with bits of lace and whalebone perhaps, was a wonder, for all its wrinkles and extra flesh. The places of extra flesh seemed derived from Elysian Fields, fruit from the garden Adam was born in. I could not help but survey it.

Cecilia Quisby smiled like a ring-dove. Her remonstration was temporarily halted so she could address this new question, the question of what she was going to do about the lust she had engendered in me.

"You don't think I'm too old and used," she said, a hint of insecurity in her voice, but a voice that quavered like a taper. She lightly spread her arms and revealed herself all the more. She was an aged Delilah, but the temptations were nonetheless irresistible.

"You're the most beautiful thing I've ever seen," I said. And I meant it.

"Come here, Todd," she said, and, of course, I did.

I stood next to the bed and she wrapped her arms around me and put her cheek on my zipper and held me there like a queen making time-honored use of some hierodule. I ran my hands over what parts I could reach—shoulders, her slightly furry cheeks, her still-glossy though graying hair, the tops of her bare breasts—but I felt as if I were straightjacketed.

What happened between Cecilia Quisby and me should not be made public knowledge. Things occurred in that plush and mirrored bedroom which I will forever want repeated, will forever be tortured for wanting them repeated. She was a remarkable woman.

After our athletic endeavors Cecilia Quisby begged off on the remainder of the evening, citing fatigue, headache, surprise, new things she would have to digest.

"Could we do this tomorrow night?" she asked from amid her pillows and silks.

I hoped for a moment she meant, well, at any rate, she meant the dinner/meeting.

"Of course," I said. I bent to kiss her on the cheek as I left and she turned slightly, I thought away from my lips, but perhaps it was just an awkward parting. I left feeling wrung out. I had at least, for the first time in a while, if only for an hour or so, forgotten *Animus* and the pledge that hung over me like the sword of Damocles. I forgot it until I arrived at Sherri's and found her in tears, her clothing torn, a bruise swelling up under her left eye like an ugly toad.

When she lifted her face to me it brought a more frantic flood of tears. She sobbed like a nun with stigmata, my name spewing from her blubbering like a curse.

"Wh-where were you?" she asked.

"Picking up Cecilia—what the hell happened?" I sat down by her and put my arms around her only to be pushed away.

"He tried to rape me, you shit," she managed to get out.

"Who?" I said, automatically, though I knew. Of course I knew.

"That beast, you selfish jackass. That goat-footed author of that horrid, horrid book. I never want to see him again. I never want to see *you* again."

"Sherri, you don't mean that," I started.

She was suddenly, fiercely calm. She looked at me with the face of an unrepentant killer about to be electrocuted.

"I do, though. I mean it. He attacked me. He thought it was part of the *deal.* God knows what goes on in that beastly mind of his. And you, while you were sporting with that rich—" Here tears took over again.

"He *told* you that, that I was bedding Cecilia Quisby?" I sputtered in mock outrage, my face coloring with shame.

"Get out, Todd. That animal tried to put his thick, dirty prick into me and I will never forget that and never forgive you for it. Get out."

I started another weak protest but I was beat. I was beat all to hell. I didn't know who I was, where I was from, who was on my side or who wasn't, or even if I was on my own side. I wandered out onto the rebarbative sidewalks and meandered around for a few hours. I was as loose as the trash blowing up Fifth Avenue. I was as pointless.

What had happened was this:

Jim Nozoufist and Cecilia Quisby, apparently in frustration over our impotence, our ignorance, our inability to get *Anima* published, had reestablished contact with Ardent Publishing and J. Quillmeier and had signed with him (in apparent disregard for the contract Nozoufist had with us, but we were weak as kittens afterward—we were cowed, subjugated—and they knew it) to bring the novel out as the sole offering from Ardent in the fall of that year. They also, coincidentally, had made a more personal, more vindictive pact to humiliate us, use us, show us that power in the circles they frequented had to do with who had whose dick. In the case of Cecilia Quisby's seduction this amounted to a fairly memorable and aristocratic, almost feline, display of how a woman controls a man, how she has him like a leopard on a leash.

In the case of the less sophisticated Jim Nozoufist this amounted to a savage attack on Sherri that included tearing her blouse and blackening her eye. Sherrifa Hoving would never press charges, for her own personal reasons, which I can only guess at. Shortly, after this, I heard she moved out west and was working for one of those fancy book houses, the ones that make a living publishing books of immaculate glossies of baby boomer memorabilia, books for *Architectural Digest* coffee tables, gorgeous books, empty as skulls. I never heard from her again.

Ironically, sadly, *Anima*, was never published. Either Cecilia Quisby and J. Quillmeier made their own secret concordat and shelved the book for reasons of their own or they came up with a better plan.

Six months later there appeared on the literary horizon a new publishing house, Quillmeier Books. Its sole first offering was a potboiler entitled *Run for It*. You know the story. It went into multiple printings, launched the publishing house making James and Cecilia Quillmeier the toasts of bookdom, sold to the Book of the Month club, went to NAL for a cool million mass-market rights, and the movie version, starring Bruce Willis and Natalie Portman, was said to be filming in Chicago, where they were having script problems which was to delay the actual release of the film until the fall of the following year.

Run for It, the book, was seemingly everywhere at once: in every chain bookstore window, in every glossy magazine's book review section, no matter how perfunctory (*People* called it "John Grisham with extra adrenaline"), in the laps of every commuter. Its author, a James Skald, had his handsome kisser spread across America like a new brand of cereal. Or a new hostage crisis; he practically had his own theme music. He was on Oprah, he was on Charlie Rose, he was on NPR.

And James Skald, household name, with a face now as familiar as Dan Rather's, seemed to have come from nowhere. He had a burnished, prizefighter's mug, somewhat ruddy, perhaps freckled (it was hard to tell through the makeup and TV lights), and his clean-shaven jaw was as chiseled and well cornered as a bank building. Still, if you squinted and held up *Time*'s cover to the right light you could see a bit of wildness there, underneath the well-groomed and artificial map. Somewhere beneath the sleek surface of that face that had been configured for television to consume and disseminate, there was something almost sinister, almost feral. It's the beast inside man, I guess. We all have it.

But, some nights, here in Pittsburgh, where I moved and got a job at another bookstore, some late nights, when I'm lonely and I'm thinking about the snake-like shapeliness of Sherri Hoving or the delights of Cecilia Quisby's venerable body, I'll pull out *Anima* and read sections of it to myself. Or aloud if I've had a couple of drinks. Or sometimes even over the phone to family or friends back home, who wonder why I've called after all these years just to spout some baffling jabber into the plastic receiver they clutch to their ears as if they expect real communication from it.

And I marvel, still, still I marvel, at the magisterial sentences, at the distilled but cockamamie wisdom, at the fantastical, magical, misbegotten, empyrean *otherness* which is this novel, *Anima*, destined to die with me, to know only the life which I bring to it.

Aftermath

Right after the crash Ralph went around talking about it as if he were the ancient mariner. "The guy came out of nowhere," is a phrase I remember from numerous renditions. It was soon reported that there was trouble at home, his still-young wife was spotted at Arby's with Jack Diamond from the church choir. Later Ralph would say he could have predicted it all, the dirty affair, the acrimony, the loss of his self-respect, and then his job. Ralph really went downhill. "The only thing I didn't see coming," Ralph was saying, "was that goddamned Plymouth."

Acknowledgements

"Monster" in _Gargoyle_

"Punk Band" in _In Posse Review_, and a piece of it in _Listen: 29 Short Conversations_ (Brown Paper Publishing, 2009)

"The Door" in _Mid-South Review_

"Blunge" in _Muse Apprentice Guild_

"Supermarket" in _Orchid_

"Killer" as an artist collaboration at Forty Forty Press

"My Friend, Bob Canaletto" in _The Edward Society_ and _Southern Voices 2_

"Delitescent Selves" in _Potomac Review_

"Strangers in Love" in _Soupletter_

"A Small Fire" in _Ghoti Magazine_, and was also nominated by them for a Pushcart

"Harry Styrene and the Holy Virgin" in _3711 Atlantic_

"The Boy who Used up a Word" in _The Melic Review_

"Notes Toward the Story" in _Cranky_

"Mike and Doris Had Everything" in _Cordite_

"Publisher" in _Eclectica_ and _Southern Gothic_, and as a chapbook from Workers Write Press

"Aftermath" in _Quick Fiction_

"Character" in _Mannequin Envy_

"Mystical Participation" in *Cellar Door*
"Haunted" in *Thirst for Fire*
"Shadow Work" in *The Pinch*
Also, "Blunge" and "Aftermath" appeared in the chapbook *Short Story and Other Short Stories* (Parallel Press, 2006)

The Afterword Gratitude: Thanks to my big brother, Mark, The Storyteller. Uncle Shlomo the Magus. To George Singleton, Dave Markson, Rick Barthelme, The Redoubtable J. Grisham, Selah S., Miles Gibson, Bob Butler, Suzanne Kingsbury, Cynthia Shearer, Debra Spark, Mark Cunningham, Tom Dyja, John Barber, Greg Downs, Pinckney Benedict, Marly Youmans, Tom Piazza, Tom Franklin, Marshall Boswell, Marshall Chapman, Lee Smith, and Richard Powers, who all made me feel welcome at the adult table. Elea Guru. Wardo the Magnificent. Special thanks to David at Blue Cubicle Press. The Gang at Burke's. My mother, Sadie Mesler, who has saved my hash too many times, and everyone else who continues to be nice to me while I roil on my own spit. And, perpetually, Cheryl, Chloe, and Toby. And a special thanks to Erin McKnight, who made me sound smarter than I am.

COREY MESLER has published in numerous journals and anthologies. He has published four novels: *Talk: A Novel in Dialogue* (2002), *We Are Billion-Year-Old Carbon* (2006), *The Ballad of the Two Tom Mores* (2010), and *Following Richard Brautigan* (2010); two full-length poetry collections: *Some Identity Problems* (2008) and *Before the Great Troubling* (2010); and two books of short stories: *Listen: 29 Short Conversations* (2009) and *Notes toward the Story and Other Stories* (2010). He has also published a dozen chapbooks of both poetry and prose. He has been nominated for the Pushcart Prize numerous times, and two of his poems have been chosen for Garrison Keillor's Writer's Almanac. He also claims to have written "The Martian Hop." With his wife, he runs Burke's Book Store, one of the country's oldest (1875) and best independent bookstores. He can be found at www.coreymesler.com.

CPSIA information can be obtained at www.ICGtesting.com
Printed in the USA
238030LV00001B/6/P